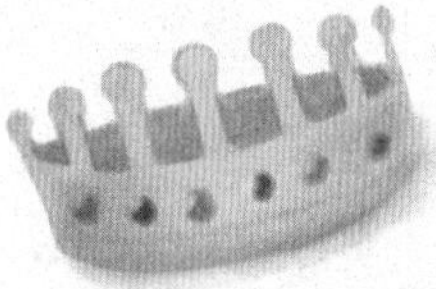

His Royal Whiskers

Also by Sam Gayton

The Adventures of Lettie Peppercorn

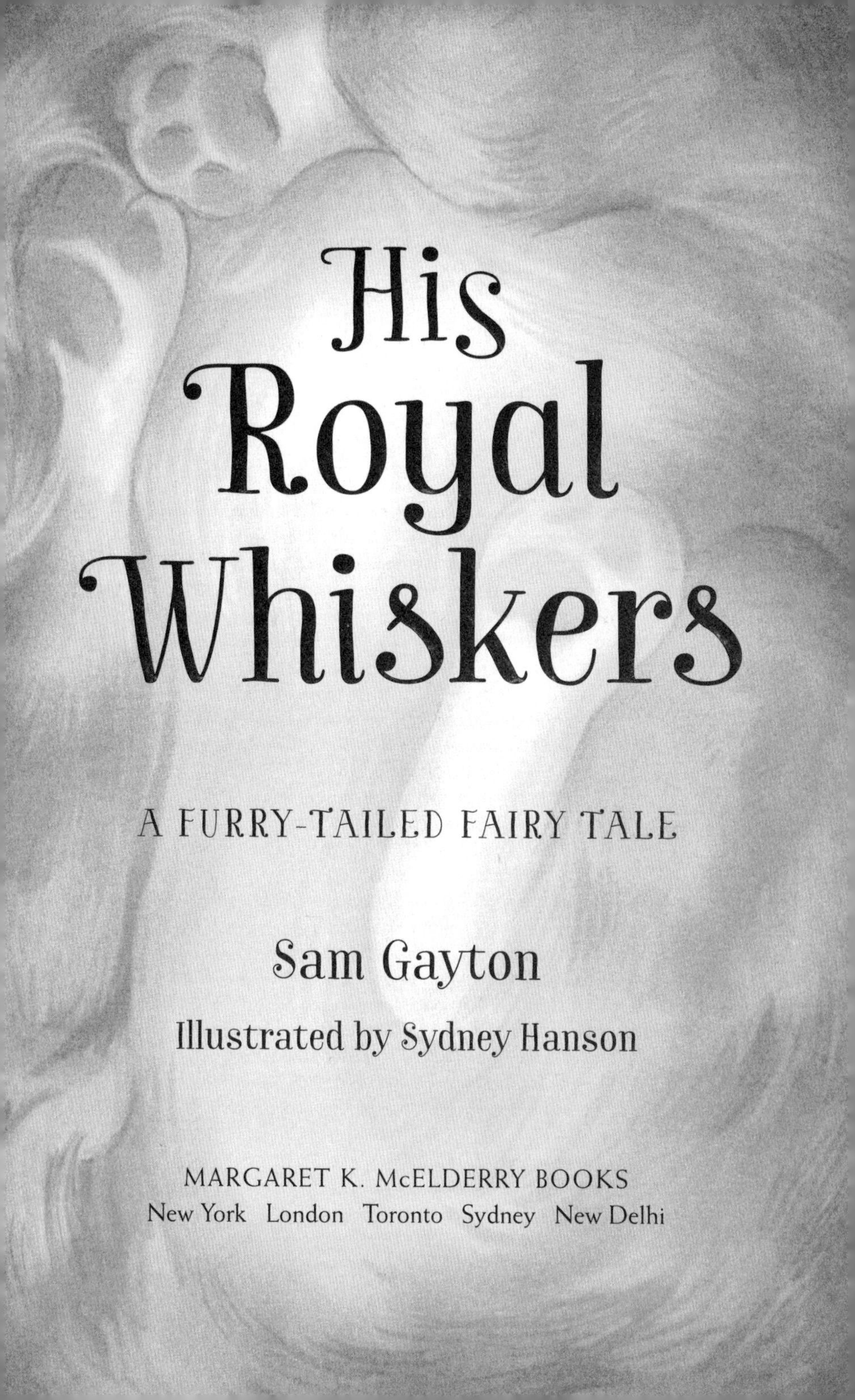

His Royal Whiskers

A FURRY-TAILED FAIRY TALE

Sam Gayton

Illustrated by Sydney Hanson

MARGARET K. McELDERRY BOOKS

New York London Toronto Sydney New Delhi

MARGARET K. McELDERRY BOOKS
An imprint of Simon & Schuster Children's Publishing Division
1230 Avenue of the Americas, New York, New York 10020
This book is a work of fiction. Any references to historical events, real people, or real places are used fictitiously. Other names, characters, places, and events are products of the author's imagination, and any resemblance to actual events or places or persons, living or dead, is entirely coincidental.

Originally published in Great Britain in 2016 by Anderson Press Ltd.
Rights licensed by arrangement with Rights People, London.
First U.S. edition 2017

Book design by Debra Sfetsios-Conover
The text for this book was set in Adobe Caslon Pro.
Manufactured in the United States of America
1017 FFG
2 4 6 8 10 9 7 5 3 1
CIP data for this book is available from the Library of Congress.
ISBN 978-1-4814-9090-0 (hardcover)
ISBN 978-1-4814-9092-4 (eBook)

For Pops, who is Tops

PART ONE
Catastrophica

I came, I saw, I conquered.

—JULIUS CAESAR

Anything that can go wrong, will go wrong.

—SOD'S LAW

(A NOTE ON NAMES)

This is a tale from Petrossia, a land far from where you or I sit now. The king there is called the Czar, which is pronounced "zar." The stories say it was actually spelled zar once too, but that was before he decided to wage war on the letter C and force it to join his name. After a long and ferocious battle, C was eventually defeated, and the victorious zar told it to march as a herald at the front of his name forever.

The letter C had to obey.

But it wasn't going to cheer about it.

So now you know why, when you say the Czar's name, the C is silent.

1

Bad News at Breakfast

Bloom and Swoon and many a moon ago, in the lands beyond the Boreal Sea, there lived a mighty king who loved conquering. He conquered crowns and cities and countries. His name was the Czar.

Conquering was the Czar's favorite hobby. He practiced all the time, so he was really rather good at it. He could conquer a whole kingdom guarded by ten thousand soldiers using nothing but a tin whistle, a fishing rod, and a herd of reindeer.[1]

---

1. This actually happened. On the first day of Bloom, the Czar had ridden north to the kingdom of Laplönd and challenged King Harollia to single combat.

Normally, of course, no king would accept such a challenge. It would be suicide. But the Czar had carried no weapons: only a tin whistle and a fishing rod.

So, arming himself with battle-ax and bommy-knocker, King Harollia accepted.

When he charged, the Czar climbed a fir tree and proceeded to play an irritating Yuletide tune very badly. The noise enraged a herd of nearby reindeer, who stampeded through the valley, sweeping King Harollia away. Up in his tree, the Czar used the fishing rod to pluck the crown from King Harollia's head as the reindeer carried him past.

He was a terrifying beast of a man—broad as a bear, strong as an ox, clever as a pig, and hairy as a goat. His burgundy boots shone, his midnight cloak swished, and his Iron Crown sat slowly rusting on his head. He could crush coconuts with his hands and do push-ups with his mustache. He was simply the mightiest conqueror of all time. Everyone agreed. And if you didn't, the Czar would fight you until you changed your mind.

One bleak morn at the end of Dismember, the Czar woke late and sat down to conquer his huge breakfast of twelve ostrich eggs. He cracked the shells first, one by one. It was his favorite part. He liked imagining they were skulls.

He dipped all his buttered soldiers, gobbled them up, then called the butler and demanded toasted reinforcements.

The butler left to inform the cooks. After a while, the doors to the chamber crashed open. On a velvet cushion by his elbow, the Winter Palace poodle wagged his tail and sat up, as the maids marched up from the kitchens, carrying a whole new battalion of toast that was buttered on both sides.

"Down, Bloodbath," growled the Czar, jabbing the poodle with his fork. "*My* breakfast."

But the Czar and his poodle were surprised by another

visitor along with the maids. It was one of the Czar's War Council. And he was carrying bad news.

The Czar's War Council was made up of five of his most powerful soldiers—and surely the bravest and toughest of them all was his Warmaster, the barbarian warrior Ugor, who stood before him now. Ugor had fought in every single one of the Czar's conquests. He had been slashed with swords, stabbed with spears, and recently poked in the eye with a chopstick.[2] But the Czar had never seen him look so afraid before. Ugor's unbandaged eye was filled with fear as he announced that a terrible catastrophe had befallen the Czar's six-year-old son and only heir—Alexander, the Prince of Petrossia.

"What do you mean, a terrible catastrophe?" scoffed the Czar, catapulting breadcrumbs out of his mouth and across the breakfast table. "Has my son been kidnapped? Ha! Kidnapping doesn't worry me in the slightest, Ugor! I will simply invade any kingdom holding him to ransom."

"No, Majesty," grunted Warmaster Ugor, turning pale. "Badder than kidnap."

"Worse than kidnapping?" cried the Czar. "You mean my son has been murdered? Then I must try to fulfill my ultimate ambition: conquer the land of the dead, and bring Alexander back from the afterlife!"

---

2. Last summer, when the Czar had surprised the Ninjas of Soy during breakfast and conquered them before lunch.

"No, Majesty." Ugor's knees were knocking together. "Badder than murder too."

"Worse than murder?" cried the Czar, and even he began to feel a little afraid. "What has happened?"

But Ugor was so overcome with terror, he fainted and toppled with a thud to the floor.

With a scowl, the Czar booted Bloodbath out from under his ankles. The poodle scampered over to the Warmaster, licking and slobbering all over Ugor's face until the barbarian regained consciousness. Finally, the Warmaster sat up and managed to inform the Czar that Prince Alexander, his only son and heir to the mighty Petrossian Empire, had somehow been transformed into a fluffy-wuffy kitten.

The blood of the Czar himself ran cold. "You mean to say that the heir to my great empire is now a . . . a . . ."

"Kitten," confirmed Ugor with a groan. "And, Majesty?"

"What?" said the Czar in the barest whisper.

"He's got fleas too."

Even Ugor—Warmaster, and bravest of the Czar's War Council—could not meet His Majesty's smoldering stare of rage.

"How?" growled the Czar. "How did this happen?"

"A potion, Majesty," Ugor said whilst hiding behind his beard.

"Alchemy?" The Czar clenched his fist until his knuckles cracked. "Who brewed and bottled it?"

"Two children," said Ugor. "Boy and girl. Lord Xin catch them. Got them in dungeons now."

"Assassins, no doubt. The Duke of Madri must have sent them on a revenge mission." The Czar glared down at Bloodbath, who whimpered and hid under the table. "I never should have kidnapped his poodle."

"Not assassins," Ugor explained. "Just children. Living here in Winter Palace. Prince Alexander's two best friends."

The Czar made the sort of face—half surprised, half disgusted—that ramblers usually make when they fail to see the cowpat.

"My son has *friends*?" said the Czar. This was getting worse and worse.

"Best friends," corrected Ugor.

"He has *best* friends?"

Ugor nodded. "Two of them."

"TWO?!"

The Czar stood up and thumped the breakfast table with his fist. He thumped it so hard that his twelve ostrich eggs bounced up from their eggcups and cracked on the floor like guillotined heads. He swept the stacks of buttered soldiers off their silver tray. All fifty of them fell facedown on the bloodred carpet. In all the Czar's life there had never been a greater proof of Sod's Law.

"This is a disaster!" he roared. "Not only is my son a kitten, but a *friendly* kitten too? This is a CATASTROPHE. How can I have a fluffy-wuffy furball for an heir? How can he command an army when he can only meow? How can he hold a sword with paws? How can he be a conqueror? HOW?!"

The Czar roared that last question so loud, his voice echoed through the entire Winter Palace, as if searching for an answer.

"How?

How?

How?

HOW?"

It echoed off walls painted eggshell blue and windows fringed with white cornices, like icing on a cake . . .

It was heard across the courtyard, in the ears of all the marble statues that made up the Fountain of Sobs: a pyramid of kings and queens conquered by the Czar, whose chiseled effigies had been plumbed up to weep an endless splish of tears . . .

It went all the way up to the gilded chimneys on the rooftop, and all the way down to the kitchens in the basement, and even farther below that, to the dungeons. . . .

Where, behind a great many locked doors, down a great many torch-lit tunnels, and in a great deal of trouble, a boy and girl sat together, trying to think of a way out.

"We're getting our heads cut off," Pieter Abadabacus said when he heard the Czar's cry echo down to them.

There in the gloom beside him, Teresa Gust shook her head. "You don't know that for sure. The Czar might have been yelling angrily for a completely different reason. Maybe he stubbed his big toe."

A second roar of rage echoed down to them.

"Both big toes," Teresa corrected.

Pieter gave her a look.

She shrugged. "It happens."

"We never should have made that potion, Teresa!" Pieter slumped his shoulders, letting his heavy lead chains clonk onto the floor. "Poor Alexander. Poor us. What was I thinking?"

That was a question Pieter would never find the answer to. He was an Abadabacus; the thirteenth in a long line of master mathemagicians; a genius who had trained in Eureka and had (at the age of four and a half) single-handedly saved that city from being destroyed by the Czar.

He had lived in the Winter Palace ever since, serving in the War Council as Petrossia's Royal Tallymaster. The Czar entrusted him with working out the most important of sums. Not only did Pieter know exactly how many men it would take to conquer North Hertzenberg (three legions, give or take a battalion), but he knew how many steps they would have to march to get there (two million), and the shoe size of every soldier in the company. He knew his *fifty-seven times table*, for infinity's sake. . . .

So why, in the name of everything odd and even, had he been so stupid as to go along with Teresa's idea?

"I've got some new escape plans!" she suddenly announced.

Pieter sighed. "Have any got a better chance of working than the eleven you've already suggested?"

Teresa gave him one of her looks (the one with the narrowed eyes and the scorn). "They had potential."

"*Infinitesimal* potential."

"I don't see *you* coming up with any ideas."

That was true. But then Pieter often left the brainstorming to Teresa. She was a completely different type of genius from him. His brain was all about answers—working them out, choosing one that was right, checking it over twice . . .

But Teresa Gust had Imagination. And Imagination was all about knowing what questions to ask in the first place.

"All right," he told her. "Let's hear your escape plans."

"What if we brew *another* potion that turns iron into chocolate? Use it on the bars of this cell, nibble through them, and make a run for it?"

"We don't have a cauldron," Pieter pointed out. "Also, you hate chocolate."

"We'll dig, then," Teresa suggested. "Find an underground river, and doggy paddle to freedom."

Pieter gestured at his uniform. Unlike Teresa, whose suit was covered with grappling hooks and color-coded patchwork pockets, his Tallymaster uniform was a plain gray suit and cloak. It included a gold T for *Tallymaster*, embroidered on his lapels, and a left sleeve made out of paper, so he could jot down equations. It did not include a shovel. Or inflatable armbands.

"All right," she said. "We befriend a mouse and ask it to steal the keys to the cell—like the old folkmother does in the *Hansa and Greta* story, when those two horrible children lock her up and start gobbling her home."

Teresa looked expectantly over at a rat skulking round the corners of her cell. She gave it a friendly wave, and held out her hand for it to shake.

"I'm in the wrong fairy tale," she huffed a moment later, sucking her bitten thumb.

Pieter had to agree. But despite everything, he laughed. How did Teresa come up with so many ideas? Where did they come from? And why did they never fail to make him smile? She was like a conjurer, drawing a never-ending rainbow scarf of notions from out of her sleeve. Even now, he could not help but shake his head in wonder.

That was the reason he was in this mess, Pieter worked out suddenly. That was why he'd started secretly brewing potions in the basement, and ended up turning Prince Alexander into a kitten. The answer was very simple:

Numbers were predictable.

Teresa Gust was not.

For example: they first became friends after she had kidnapped him.

(A NOTE ON TIME)

We're going back in time now, to the month when Pieter and Teresa first met. Perhaps it would have been simpler to start at the start, but this is a tale about two geniuses, and Pieter and Teresa have never in their lives done anything the easy way.

So, in your mind, see the days going backward. Imagine the brown Dismember leaves drifting upward, fixing themselves back onto the bare branches of the trees, growing green again and scrunching up into buds. Imagine the salmon of Swoon swimming north again, up the River Ossia, fish tails first, like silver needles unstitching the water. Imagine the smell of spring blossom, and the kitchen shelves creaking with the weight of apricots, artichokes, and chives.

Stop there. Don't go back any farther than Bloom. Calendars in Petrossia are only seven months long. Spring and summer stick around for a month each, and autumn lingers for two, before a long winter comes howling down from the Waste in the north to swallow up the rest of the year. There is a rhyme the Petrossia folk tell their children, and here it is:

Springtime is Bloom,
Summer is Swoon,
Autumn is Sway and Dismember,
Winter is Welkin and Worsen and Yule—
I've told you, so now you'll remember.

2

Pieter + Teresa = Trouble

One night in Bloom, three months past, before Dismember turned the leaves brown and the geese south and the Prince of Petrossia furry, Pieter woke up in the middle of the night and found he was not in his bed but in a large black sack.

"What's going on?" he mumbled. "Where am I?"

His genius brain answered him at once with a few possibilities. Pieter chose the most statistically probable option.

"Somebody help!" he yelled. "I think I've sleepwalked into a garbage bag!"

(This happened more often than you might think. Pieter had a habit of pacing back and forth—both while he worked, and while he dreamed.)

From somewhere, he heard the creak of pulleys. The bag was winching slowly upwards. Hopefully this wasn't the conveyer belt to the Winter Palace's garbage incinerator.

"Help!" he called again.

"Quiet!" hissed a voice. "Aren't you supposed to be a genius?"

"Aren't you supposed to be helping me out of this garbage bag?" Pieter answered.

There was a sigh from outside. "Are you really a mathemagician? Because you sound like an idiot."

(Like many of the finest mathemagical geniuses, Pieter could be either, depending on the subject.)

"Of course I'm a mathemagician," he said indignantly. "Test me if you want."

There was a pause. "What's the square root of ninety one thousand, two hundred and four?"

"Three hundred and two," Pieter answered.

"Umm . . . correct," decided the voice. "Probably."

Before Pieter could reply, the sack opened, and he was falling. He clonked onto a wooden floor and looked around with bleary eyes.

He was not in his tallychamber, with its dust and tinderlamp and endlessly multiplying spiders. There were no censuses, no records, no surveys around him. No stack of Tallymaster tasks, no stove where Pieter threw scrunched-up paper all scribbled with sums, no list detailing how many horseshoes the Czar had in total (both lucky and unlucky).

Pieter was down in the palace kitchens, on one of the enormous shelves that rose up and crisscrossed each basement wall, like tree branches. It was a jungle down here. The air was a hot damp fog of spicy aromas and steam. Down on the floor below, orange fires purred in their stoves like sleeping tigers, while great swamps of porridge bubbled and burped in pans, ready for tomorrow's breakfast.

But the cooks and the maids were all in bed. Pieter glanced down at the grandpapa clock *ticktocking* by the double doors. Its hands pointed at three of the morn.

"Took you down the chimney, in case you're wondering," said the voice. "All the fireplaces connect together. Hidden passages, if you think about it. Quick and secret. Not very clean though. Sorry about the soot, by the way."

Pieter looked down at his filthy pajamas.

Then around at the girl standing behind him.

Being a genius, Pieter was used to figuring people out within a matter of moments. They were like puzzles he could solve. The Czar, for example, was clearly an evil tyrant with ambitions for world-domination (it was the mustache that gave him away).

The girl Pieter found himself face to face with, though, confounded him—like a sum that didn't add up right. She was a short, plait-tailed serf in a coat made of pockets, yet somehow she equaled more than that. Pieter couldn't solve the proud angle of her chin, or measure the length of her moon-white hair, or the depth of her eyes, the color of morn stars. Her smile was an enigma. It had suddenly appeared on her face, and he had no idea why. Nor did he understand why he found himself grinning along with her, as if she was an equation he had to balance out.

"Teresa Gust," she said, thrusting her hand out. "Spice Monkey. Serf. And right now, I suppose, Kidnapper."

"Pieter Abadabacus." He took her hand and she yanked him to his feet. "Royal Tallymaster and Mathemagician."

"And Hostage," Teresa reminded him.

"And Hostage," Pieter agreed.

He really ought to have worked it out sooner. Pieter had been predicting a kidnapper, a black sack, and a snatching in the dead of night for some time now. As the best Tallymaster on the continent, he was constantly being told—often by Lord Xin during War Council meetings—that the Czar's enemies would one day try to capture him and use his mathemagical abilities for their own ends.

"Are you going to ransom me?" he asked Teresa, trying to work it out. "Did the Duke of Madri send you? Is this revenge for his poodle?"

"No, no, and no," Teresa said. "You ask a lot of stupid

questions for a genius. Maybe you'll be smarter if I wake you up a bit." She thrust a mug of something hot and earthy into his hand. "Sip this. Three teaspoons of khave, half a nib of sugarcane, and a smidge of blazing pip."

Pieter sipped it experimentally. The khave was sweet and smoky. It tingled on his tongue, and behind his eyes. He instantly felt more awake. And then more confused.

"Why have you carried me down here, then?" he asked.

"Carrying is what I do." The girl pointed to her suit.

It was covered with grappling hooks and color-coded patchwork pockets with little labels: peppercorn, parsley, and blazing pip chili.

It took Pieter a moment to understand. "Oh!" he said suddenly. His kidnapper was the kitchen's Spice Monkey—a serf who had the job of climbing around the kitchen walls like a mountaineer, gathering up and tossing down whatever ingredients the cooks needed from the shelves to sprinkle in their dishes.

"Want to play a game of hide-and-seek?" Teresa asked.

Pieter's bewilderment multiplied by a factor of ten. The mug of khave had been odd. Hide-and-seek was even odder. (What a stupid phrase, he thought. How could something be both even and odd?)

"Well?" Teresa said. "Do you?"

Pieter hesitated. This really wasn't what he'd imagined when Lord Xin and Ugor had warned him about kidnappers. Perhaps it was a dreadful trick. Maybe he should just scream and struggle until he was rescued.

On the other hand, hide-and-seek was his favorite game. It was the only one the mathemagicians in Eureka had allowed him to play, because it involved counting.[3]

"You geniuses sure need a lot of thinking time," Teresa said loudly. "You playing or not?"

Since he was Teresa's hostage, and since it wouldn't be clever to refuse his kidnapper's demands, and since Pieter always made the smart choice, he agreed.

(It had nothing to do with the fact that no one had asked him to play a game for years, or that his mug of khave was delicious, or that he was having rather a nice time being kidnapped. And it certainly had nothing to do with Teresa's uncountable freckles, or the way that even her scowls made Pieter's head giddy but not with numbers, and his heart start beating faster than he could count.)

"All right," he said, hoping the moonlight was too weak for her to see his blushes. "Let's play."

---

3. Most children in hide-and-seek only count to threnty, but when Pieter played it with his tutors, he would have to count out his fifty-seven times table, or pi to a million decimal places.

Teresa led Pieter from shelf to shelf. She harnessed him to the climbing ropes that dangled down in front of each ledge like jungle vines. Each one was color-coded for where it would take you: yellow for the bread shelf, red for the cured meats, purple for the wine racks.

Teresa hooked them both to the green rope. Pieter barely had time to shut his eyes before she had tipped them both over the edge. Together they swung like monkeys across the kitchen. Pieter's stomach soared into his chest and his feet kicked in the empty air, while Teresa held him tight and laughed into the wind.

Their feet touched down on the next shelf, they skidded to a stop and unclipped the harness, and Pieter opened his eyes to see where the green rope had led them.

It was the part of the kitchen where the herbs were kept. Lush swishing plants sprouted out of rows of crates like green jack-in-the-boxes. Dill, sage, and mint filled the moonlit air with their crisp sweet smells. Pieter took a deep breath and sighed. He hadn't known that such a beautiful place could exist in the cold, regal splendor of the Winter Palace. The herb garden was as peaceful and secluded as a mountain meadow. It was wonderful.

"You seek and I'll hide," Teresa told him, then ran off with a rustle into the leaves.

Closing his eyes, Pieter counted: "Twenty-seven, twenty-eight, twenty-nine, threnty! You asked for time, and I've given you plenty!"

He called out the start-searching rhyme, then listened hard for any sounds in reply. He couldn't hear anything but the herbs whispering to one another, and the echoing drips of the kitchen taps far below.

He started sifting through the sage and dill. Then he went to the spice boxes, opening them up like presents, and letting out a disappointed huff when he peeked inside each one.

Biscuit crates. Old plates. Barrels of hazelnuts and wrinkly dates. He searched stacks and racks and behind the backs of piled-up sacks. He saw rats the size of cats and glittering emerald roaches as big as broaches, munching on food forgotten or gone rotten . . .

But no Teresa Gust.

Not a rustle nor a giggle nor a scamper of footsteps.

Where was she?

He was about to call out the give-up rhyme ("Count from threnty back to one, come out now because you've won!") when Pieter realized that he could just run away. He could climb down the shelf, find Ugor or Lord Xin, and get his kidnapper thrown into the dungeons.

He ought to do just that. It was what a loyal servant of

Petrossia would do. (And he *was* a loyal servant. It would not be a smart choice to make the Czar start to question that. . . .)

Pieter looked over at the color-coded rope he'd been winched up on. Maybe he'd just have one last look.

He crept back to the herb garden and went over to the rosemary. It was wildly overgrown—as thick as a hedgerow. He had to bend several branches back like catapults and squeeze through quick, before they went *twang* and sent him flying.

He crawled in farther. It was so dark, he almost head-butted the basement wall. It rose up like a sheer cliff, and there in the bricks . . .

"What are *they*?" he murmured to himself.

If Pieter hadn't been playing hide-and-seek, he would have missed the handholds completely. They were cut roughly into the wall—a trail of divots that small hands could grip onto and climb up. When Pieter saw what they were leading up to, he gave a triumphant grin.

There was a sliding trapdoor in the shelf above.

On it, someone with very bad handwriting had chalked the words:

FORBIDDEN DOOR—

DO NOT ENTER

(A NOTE ON FORBIDDEN DOORS)

Forbidden doors are subject to the same universal law that governs envelopes stamped with the words TOP SECRET, or boxes entrusted to little girls called Pandora. It is not a question of *if* they get opened, but how much trouble comes out *when* they are.

Looking up at the trap door, Pieter could imagine Teresa crouched behind it, giggling to herself in her secret hiding hole. What he could not imagine was the trouble that was also behind it—trouble beyond all measure and counting—just waiting for some stupid genius to let it out.

3

The Alchemist's Assistant

Quickly, Pieter climbed from handhold to handhold until he reached the trap door. He counted a silent one, two, three—then wrenched it open.

"Found you!" he cried, sticking his head inside.

His triumph quickly faded. He had found something, all right—and not just his kidnapper. Teresa stood in the middle of a narrow room, waiting for him. She had built a little hidden den by stacking boxes away from the wall, making a hollow space between the crates and bricks.

A secret shelf.

"Come on up," she said, her face serious.

Teresa's secret shelf was stuffy and dark. A few tinderflies sat tied to the stumps of sugarsticks, wings glimmering with golden light as they snoozed. Dim as it was, Pieter could still make out the mess. There were stoppered bottles everywhere—bundled, piled, stacked, clustered, and clumped together. He'd never seen such strange-looking herbs and spices.

Stranger still were the walls: they were chalked from floor to ceiling with words, as if they were gigantic pages. The writing had been scribbled out, rubbed off, and rewritten. It was linked together with arrows; emphasized with circles; ridiculed with question marks.

Then he saw the cauldron.

Suddenly Pieter realized the secret shelf was a *laboratory* of some sort. The bottles around him were ingredients, and the writing was instructions. He had discovered Teresa (or she had let him find her) in the middle of cooking up something. And it wasn't a cake.

"I wasn't totally honest with you before," Teresa told him. "I'm a Spice Monkey, a serf, your kidnapper . . . But I want to be something else too. Something special. Something *more*. I dream about it every night and think about it every day, the way you must dream about numbers." She took a deep breath. "I'm learning to be an alchemist."

Alchemy. A shiver ran up Pieter's spine and set his brain trembling in his skull. He didn't know much about alchemy: only that it was forbidden, dangerous, and even more unpredictable than Teresa was. It was the science of change. The magic of metamorphosis. The theory of transformation. Alchemical potions *changed* things. (In Pieter's experience, usually for the worse.)

"I'm learning to be an alchemist," she said again. "I want to make a potion. And I need *you* to help me brew it, Pieter. That's why I brought you here. That's why I showed you all this."

Pieter took a step backwards. In a small voice, he said: "I think I'd like to go back in that garbage bag now, please."

"Pieter—"

"Alchemy is forbidden, unless by royal decree! And even then, it's too dangerous! Do you know how many laboratories we have in the Winter Palace?"

Teresa nodded. "One. At the top of the North Spire. With the roof that looks like a wizard's hat. Right?"

"Wrong!" said Pieter. "That's only *half* a laboratory. The last Royal Alchemaster we had blew it up. He was on the War Council with me. His name was Blüstav. It was his job to invent potions that would turn lead into gold and tin into silver, to pay for all the Czar's armies. But now Blüstav's been banished—all five hundred and sixty-three pieces of him."

Teresa turned a little pale in the gloom. "He blew himself to bits?"

"Almost as bad: he accidentally turned himself into a pile

of coins. Fourteen roubles and ninety-eight kopeks he came to altogether, once I'd added him up. The Czar piled him up in a sack and used him to buy a siege cannon."

"So . . . there's a job opening?" Teresa said brightly.

Pieter groaned. "You don't understand. . . ."

"Neither do you!" she suddenly thundered. "You think I want to be a Spice Monkey all my life? Just fetching and carrying, until I'm old and stooped? No! It's wrong. Why should I be a serf? Why should anyone?"

"Because the Czar only gives you two choices," Pieter said. "You can be a serf, or a head on a spike."

"But I'm not asking *him*, Pieter. I'm asking *you*!"

All at once the anger drained out of her. Teresa Gust was just like the weather in spring, Pieter was beginning to realize. She could thunder—she could howl and spit hail. But her black moods never lasted, and before long she'd be bright and sunny again.

"I can do alchemy," Teresa explained. "I *can*. I just haven't got it out of my imagination and into real life yet. That's why I need you. How can I put it into words . . ." She tugged at her white plait, like it was a bell pull to her brain, and she was requesting an explanation from it. "It's like I'm trying to bake a cake," she said. "I know I need flour, and I know I need butter, but I don't know the amounts. You can tell me,

Pieter. You'll know *how much*—that's what you mathemagicians are good at, isn't it? So I can say 'flour,' and you can tell me 'three bags full.' I'll say 'butter,' and you'll say 'half that block.' It'll be just like that. You see?"

"But if the Czar finds out you're doing *alchemy* . . ." Pieter didn't finish. It didn't matter. They both knew how it would end: with the subtraction of heads from shoulders.

"We'll work at night," Teresa said. "Here on the secret shelf. I'll grapple up the chimney. Fetch you like I did tonight. You'll be back in your bunk before sunrise, and no one will know. Not the cooks, not the Czar . . . no one but us." She caught hold of his hand. "It'll be a secret."

Pieter's heart beat faster. He was already hooked on sharing things with Teresa: games of hide-and-seek, cups of khave . . . now she was offering him a secret. A secret that held the promise of *more* sharing. Of midnight meet-ups, and yawning at dawn, and next to no sleep, standing side by side.

"But what potion would we make?" Pieter's head filled with a near infinite list of problems. "How long would it take? Why . . ." He trailed off. "Why are you smiling?"

Teresa clapped her hands together in delight. "You're asking questions, Pieter. That means you want answers. And *that* means you're going to help me find them."

Pieter blushed. It was true. Teresa was an enigma, but she'd solved him like the simplest of sums. Just give him a problem—what else could he do but solve it?

"You're not going to *use* our alchemy on anyone, are you?" he asked suddenly. "You don't want to commit murder, or . . . or do anything traitorous, or forbidden, or anything like that?"

For just a moment, a strange green light flashed in her eyes. But then she blinked, and fixed him with her widest, starriest stare. "Hand on heart, Pieter—I don't want to murder *anyone*."

(It occurred to Pieter much later that this wasn't a full answer to everything he'd asked. But at the time, he just sighed.)

"Do you have a recipe?" he said. "You *do* have a recipe?"

Teresa shrugged. "Got a million." She tapped her head. "All made up on my own. Let me tell you some, and you can work out which one is the least likely to explode."

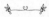

They stayed up on the secret shelf until the grandpapa clock chimed five, nibbling sugar lumps and chewing pepperleaf, putting their heads together for the first time and finding that they fit each other perfectly, like long-lost bits of the same jigsaw. When Teresa took him back to his tallychamber at dawn, Pieter searched for his list, nine hundred items long, of all the things in Petrossia that were simply better when put together. Below the nine hundredth entry ("Peace conferences and arsenic"), Pieter took up his quill and wrote in his tiny, careful handwriting:

901. Pieter Abadabacus and Teresa Gust.

"We're more when you add us up, and less when we're divided," he whispered to himself. "It's just basic mathemagics, really."

He was exhausted, but too exhilarated to sleep, so Pieter put down his quill and went to the Groansday Book—a thick encyclopedia chained up with lead that contained a list of every slave in Petrossia.

He wanted to find out everything he could about Teresa—where was she from? How old was she? How long had she been here at the Winter Palace? Would she respond well to flowers and chocolate?

He jabbed his finger on the page and scrolled down the list. He passed his own entry (*1137: Pieter Abadabacus, Royal Tallymaster. Born and conquered in Eureka. Age: 11*), got to the last name and frowned.

He checked again.

And a third time, just to be sure.

There she was! Sixteen entries ahead of him in the Groansday Book. He'd skipped over her because her record was incomplete. *1121: Teresa Gust, Kitchen Spice Monkey. Age: 12.*

Pieter chained up the book again, and heaved it back onto its shelf. Teresa had no place of birth or conquering. Perhaps she had been born amongst the wildfolk, who lived in little painted trundle-wagons out in the Western Woodn't.[4] Sleeping beneath the sky turned their hair moon white and their eyes the color of starlight, just like Teresa's. Some of them even had power to change things too, or so the stories said.

"Like in *Cindestrella*," he murmured to himself. "Where the fairy folkmother turns nine brides into a horse-drawn carriage, so they can ride away from the wicked prince who wants to marry them all."

But the wildfolk were roamers—just one of the many peoples that traveled across the continent. If Teresa was truly one of them, why was she here? Where had she come from?

Pieter would ask Teresa that question many times. From spring to summer, as Bloom became Swoon, and on into Sway, she would always answer the same way: cryptically.

---

4. The Western Woodn't lies at the edge of Petrossia's border. It is a bit like a wood, only bigger, darker, wilder . . . and hungrier.

"Where was I born? Bloom and Swoon and many a moon ago, in a land beyond the first and last."

Sometimes, he'd pressed her for more. "Where is that, though? Madri? The Western Woodn't?"

"I'm from the moon, Pieter. I'm a lunar baby."

"You're a lunatic, more like. Are you one of the wildfolk? Is that why your hair is white?"

"All right," she'd say. "This is the truth—I'm an old bald monkey born up the top of a palm tree. A big gale blew me down the chimney."

"That explains why you're so good at climbing. And the smell."

She'd laugh and give him a playful punch. "Enough natter, Pieter. We need to get to work!"

And Pieter would work, thinking all the while, but not about the potion. He'd think about Teresa, and how she was not only a genius at asking questions, but avoiding them too.

There was so much to do. First, Pieter and Teresa had to decide what potion to make. They did this by a process of elimination. Teresa began by examining her collection of alchemical ingredients—pilfered from the kitchen shelves over years and years.[5]

5. It might surprise you that Teresa could locate such a plethora of unusual substances from what was essentially a large kitchen larder. But there is almost nothing in this world that someone, somewhere does not class as a delicacy.

Then she would begin: drawing idea after idea from her mind, the way magicians can draw rabbits from their hats, or eggs from behind ears, or pocket watches from handkerchiefs they have just whacked with a hammer only moments before.

"What about a potion that turns you back into a baby? Or a tonic that can shrink whoever drinks it? Could we mix up an elixir with the power to turn things into cats?"

Pieter paced back and forth, working out each potion's chances mathemagically, until finally he would declare it:

"Dangerous."

Or, "*Extremely* dangerous."

Until finally, at last, he said: "Wait a second. That last one could work."

Teresa stared at him. "An elixir with the power to turn things into cats? Really?"

Pieter double-checked the figures in his head. "Really," he said. "It's risky, it's half crazy, there are several million uncertainties . . . But yes. It could work. It might even be useful. There *are* a lot of rats on these shelves. And if we do something helpful, it might help us if the Czar finds out."

Teresa's mouth hung open. Her half-chewed pepperleaf fell out.

"Finally," she said. "We have a recipe."

"A good recipe," said Pieter.

"A *great* recipe."

"Now all we need is a name."

Three khaves and a pepperleaf later, they had it.

Teresa chalked it up on the wall:

CATASTROPHICA

Dusk until dawn in the cramped little laboratory. Tired days and frantic nights, giddy with secret alchemy. Crowding around the cauldron fire, dizzy with the heat. Boil it up and simmer it down. Pieter's pacing, Teresa's frown. Mix it all together and whirl it all apart. *Something isn't working.* Go back to the start.

How do we get whiskers to grow? *Try whisking the potion, then add the whisk?* Give it a try—what's the risk . . .

Fizzle, sizzle, hiss, spit—*Look out!*—BOOM! Wave away the fumes. *When will it work?* Soon . . .

Stir in clover, fold in cream. Pause and stir, pause and stir. Pause four times, to make four paws. The tips of kitchen knives for claws. A hundred other things and more.

Boil it down to syrupy gloop. Thicker than soup, thicker than stew, thicker than porridge, thick as glue. Make it glop and gunk and guck. Just one drop will be enough. This stuff is seriously strong! It'll change things for a long, long, *long* time.

Do you think maybe we should make it weaker . . . ? Don't be silly—make it *stronger*, Pieter!

All spring and summer, that's how it went.

The Great, Furry Experiment.

Of course, an experiment was all it was for Pieter. The time when the Catastrophica might actually *work* was a far-off moment he had barely thought about yet. Sometimes, he would dream of the day they rid the kitchens of rats. Teresa would be promoted to Alchemaster, and sit on the War Council beside him . . .

But mostly, Pieter was too distracted by the second, secret alchemy that was changing his heart whenever Teresa smiled at him. For uncountable in number are the many alchemicals in this world, but most common and powerful of them all is love.

4

Alexander Turns Six

On the day of the catastrophe, Prince Alexander was woken in his bed by the dawn peeking through the drawn curtains. It was five of the morn. The last week of Dismember. Today he was six years old.

He sat up, rubbing his eyes. Through the crack in the curtains, the sun had sent him a present. A thin stem of light lay across his quilt like a golden rose. The prince reached out to touch it. The light was warm and luminous on his fingers. Mama had loved flowers—mintflower most of all. Teresa had told him that.

He slid out of his bed and into his slippers. Hugging his nightgown around him, he tiptoed to his door. Father's present was in the enormous birthday stocking that hung from the handle. It was wrapped in red polka-dot paper the color of blood splatter. Alexander could already tell what it was from the shape. He tried not to feel disappointed.

Another crossbow.

He unwrapped it half-heartedly (but carefully—in case it was loaded). Then he lugged the crossbow over to his weapons rack and left it with the others. It looked identical to last year's crossbow, and the one from the year before that. A little bigger, maybe. Like him. Today he was six years old, not five. He had one more crossbow. Nothing else had changed. Mama would always be gone.

Alexander always thought of her on this day. The Czarina had died just after he'd been born. His life began just as hers began to end. Now she was buried outside the Winter Palace, in the Chapel of the Frozen Tear. The Czar had ordered her coffin made from ice and æther, so that he could always peer in at her frozen beauty.

Alexander often went to see her, but only in the evenings. In the rosy sunset light, he could sometimes fool himself. *She is only sleeping. She is only sleeping.* He'd whisper it to himself, over and over, then go back to his room and look at the pictures of Spring Beauty in his fairy tale books.

"You know what always makes me feel better when I'm sad? Cake. Always works. Without fail."

The voice was just a whisper. It echoed, as if it was inside Alexander's head, but it came from the empty fireplace behind him. He turned to face the chimney flue. His joint-best friend's face had appeared in its usual place.

Alexander couldn't remember a time when Teresa hadn't popped up from the fireplace. She had just always been there. He supposed that's why she was his joint-best friend. Because he couldn't imagine life without her.

"Did you say cake?" he asked Teresa.

"That's right." Teresa's head poked out from behind the hearth. She nodded. "Cake."

"With cocoa sprinkles?" Alexander asked. "And jam in the middle? And cream?"

Teresa looked offended that he would even feel the need to ask such obvious questions. "All that and more, Your Majesty," she said, scrambling out into the fireplace and giving him an exaggerated bow. "You forgot the six tinder-sticks on top. It is your birthday, after all."

Alexander smiled for the first time that day.

"Come on down to the kitchens, then," she said, holding out a grapple and harness. "We've got baking to do."

Alexander started forward—but his worries stopped him. "What if Papa wakes?" he whispered.

Teresa pulled a face. "Don't worry about the Czar."

But Alexander did worry. He wasn't brave like Teresa—especially in matters concerning his father. "He'll want me to practice my war skills with Lord Xin."[6]

"The Czar won't even know you've left your bed," Teresa interrupted. "My friend Amna is the maid who sweeps His Majesty's room. I got her to sneak an extra sprig of snoozeweed in his samovar last night before bed. Pieter says there's a ninety-seven percent chance he'll sleep past noon."

Alexander's worries went at once. Pieter's percentages could always be trusted. He could work out the solution to any sum quicker than Alexander could copy it out of the answers book. He was the joint-cleverest joint-best friend Alexander had ever had.

Not that he had ever had any other friends apart from Pieter and Teresa. The Czar did not approve of them—in Papa's opinion, Alexander needed only soldiers and serfs.[7]

"Life isn't about making friends," Papa liked to say often. "Life is about making enemies! And then defeating them, and enslaving them, and making them sweep your halls and cook your meals! If I ever find you've made any friends, I shall spike their heads on the gatehouse wall!"

That was why Alexander doubled back to the door and

---

6. Lord Xin, the Heirmaster, was the member of the Czar's War Council responsible for tutoring Alexander. He did not teach his pupil any stories, or languages, or history—conquerors did not need such things. Instead Alexander learned how to lay siege to a fort, and when to order a cavalry charge, and the advantages and disadvantages of napalm.

7. And crossbows. You really never could have too many crossbows.

pressed his ear to the keyhole. Just to be totally sure his father was asleep.

What he heard made him smile. The Czar lay in his bedchambers across the hall, conquering the silence with his snores. Alexander left him there. He stepped into the fireplace, then slipped and clipped the harness into place. Teresa took hold of him—they both swayed above the pitch-black tunnel of the flue. Then she released the grapple and together they went whooshing down the chimney.

5

The Baking of the Birthday Cake

The kitchen was a jungle, as usual. The air was a thick soup of steam, sweat, and suds. Pans hissed and spat, and tall stacks of messy dishes grew up from the sinks, fast as bamboo. The Royal Chef yelled across the worktops as she checked each dish, her cries strange and harsh as a tropical bird's:

"More quill wheat!"

"Less dill!"

"Don't overcook the marrowfoot!"

All around, the fat cooks blundered around the stoves like oliphants, readying breakfast. In the muggy air, their top halves were hidden. Only their huge legs and white flapping aprons and gigantic bottoms could be seen.

None of them noticed Alexander and Teresa land in the unlit hearth—*poof!* The basement fireplace coughed them out in a cloud of soot.

Quickly, before they were spotted, Teresa unlatched her grapple and hurried Alexander over to the shelves. In the herb garden, Pieter stood waiting to pull them up. They rose with a *whoosh*, jerked to a stop, and stepped off the winch.

Pieter looked from Teresa to Alexander, counting up each of their soot smudges, and sighed.

"You both go down the same chimney," he said. "So why does Teresa come out ten times more covered in soot? One day I'll figure it out."

Teresa shrugged, and shook the soot off her, the way a dog shakes off fleas. "Some questions you'll never solve, Tallymaster."

"Like the question of where you're from, you mean?"

"How many times do I have to tell you? I'm a gingerbread girl who got bored of sitting up on the shelf with the other cakes."

Alexander stood still while Pieter got out a little mouse-whisker brush and cleaned all evidence of soot from the prince's dressing gown with a brisk *brush-brush*. It was very important that no one found out about the chimney. It was their secret corridor to one another. It was how they had become friends in the first place. Without it, Teresa would never have been able to kidnap Pieter, or visit Alexander in his room. Their friendship had all come from that chimney.

Which just goes to show that you can find hope anywhere. Even in a hearth full of ashes, long after you thought the fire had gone out.

"Now remember," said Pieter, once Alexander was neat again. "If we're spotted down here, there'll be trouble."

Alexander gave a solemn nod. "That's why we've got a plan in case we get spotted."

"Which is?" said Pieter, who was fond of springing tests on the prince.

Alexander scrunched up his face with concentration. "I say I was playing sieges, and I charged down the stairs and got lost."

"And?"

"And I ordered you to lead me back upstairs."

"One hundred percent correct." Satisfied, Pieter turned to Teresa and nodded.

"What do you want to bake, Alexander?" she asked. "Trifle? A St. Katerina Sponge?"

Alexander licked his lips. "I don't mind," he said. "As long as we make it together."

So that is what they did. First, Alexander made the suggestions:

"Vanilla!"

"Meringue!"

"Jelly beans!"

Then, Pieter decided the amounts:

"Three pods."

"Egg whites—use ostrich."

"Half raspberry, half strawberry."

Finally, Teresa scrabbled up the shelves to gather all the ingredients together. Her long braided hair swung like a pendulum as she worked. From a tall pot, she plucked long black vanilla beans like burned matches. An egg the size of a football was lowered down in an elastic net. Little leather bags of spice were tossed out from the billows of steam, landing perfectly at their feet.

Then, once everything was set, they started mixing.

Cooking was like magic to Alexander. All the ingredients got swirled together in a bowl the size of a cauldron. Crack the eggs, scrape the vanilla beans, sift the flour, mush the butter. Teresa went down on the winch and took the cake to the ovens, while Alexander and Pieter watched with a pair of scopical glasses. The cake went in as a tray of gloop, then the grandpapa clock chimed threnty past six, and it came out changed into a block of golden scrumptiousness.

They rode the green rope up to the herb garden and feasted on it there. Teresa lay out a picnic blanket, then covered the cake with icing and sweets.

"Happy birthday, Alexander," Teresa said. "Now you are six!"

"Or," said Pieter, "if you look at it another way, you're four hundred and thirty-eight."

Alexander scrunched up his face. "Am not!"

"You are," Pieter said. "If you count in weeks instead of years. You see? Things can seem short or long, depending on what you use to measure them."[8]

"Some wildfolk count their age by the miles they've traveled," said Teresa as she decorated the cake. "One of their queens, Babapatra, lived to over a million."

Alexander considered this for a while. So did Pieter. He didn't ask, though, how Teresa knew such things. He would only receive a riddle for an answer.

"How old am I in *days*?" Alexander asked him.

"Two thousand, one hundred and ninety-one," Pieter said instantly. "If you include the leap day."

"Two thousand, one hundred and ninety-one." Alexander grinned. "How are you so good at numbers, Pieter?"

"If you're born in Eureka, you have to be. The city is famous for its mathemagicians."

Alexander watched Pieter stick six sugarsticks in the

---

8. Some of you might be scratching your heads, saying to yourself: Pieter's mathemagics are wrong. Alexander is only 313 weeks old! But remember that a week in Petrossia is only five days long—the Czar killed off the weekend a long time ago.

cake. A tinderfly was tied to each one. "So why did you leave?

"I had to. To save the city from the Czar."

Alexander was wide-eyed. "You beat Papa in a fight?"

"Single-handedly," Pieter said with a grin. "Aged four and a half."

That was not quite the whole story. But Pieter liked keeping the details vague. It sounded like a fairy tale then. It made it seem as if he'd been some super-powered invincible toddler, who had waddled up and hit the Czar with a flying karate kick.

In actual fact, the Eurekans had spotted the Czar's army marching on the city. After quickly calculating their chances of survival (slim to none), they surrendered completely. In a decision that Pieter had never known the Czar to make before or since, he agreed to spare them, but only if they provided him with a mathemagician as tribute. Pieter's parents offered up him.

"I still can't believe you're not *angry* about that!" Teresa said with a sniff. "They gave you up to be a *slave*!"

"One boy to save a whole city?" Pieter shrugged. "That's not monstrous, it's smart."

(Though in his heart, down in the part where mathemagics made no sense, Pieter was angry. It *did* hurt. Parents were supposed to find their children more precious than anything else, weren't they? He bet Teresa's parents would have died to protect her. Maybe they had. Perhaps that's why she didn't talk about them.)

"They handed you over as if you were a purse of old pennies," Teresa muttered. "And I think you're worth more than all the treasure there is."

Pieter smiled at that, but shook his head all the same. Sometimes, he didn't understand Teresa at all. She said things that just didn't add up. But the strangest thing of all was, he couldn't shake the feeling she was somehow right.

Alexander made his wish and cut the wicks on each tinderstick, freeing the six little living flickers of flame. The tinderflies flew up and away like sparks from a fire. They carried your wishes up to the stars, so it was said.

Teresa took out the knife and cut three huge slices. The birthday cake was so hot it burned Alexander's fingers, and so sweet it hurt his baby teeth. He sat there, belly full and heart bursting, trying to remember the last time he had felt so happy.

"Teresa's right," he said, spraying crumbs everywhere. "Cake does help."

Pieter was halfway through his second slice when, over by the shelf edge, Teresa shrieked.

It was the sort of shriek that, when uttered in a kitchen, could have meant several things. Maybe she had just seen a particularly huge rat scurry over the shelves, or accidentally set fire to a tea towel. Pieter couldn't smell smoke, so a rat was most likely. He turned to see if he was correct.

"We've been spotted!" Teresa hissed, leaping back from the edge. She kicked the birthday cake into the mint bushes, then grabbed up the picnic blanket and shoved it inside a crate of breadsticks. "Remember what you say, Alexander! You got lost and we found you and we're definitely not friends."

Pieter scrambled up to his feet, heart pounding, belly full of cake. Down in the kitchen below was a man slender as a willow cane, with skin smooth as porcelain and eyes the color of jade. A cloak of midnight velvet hung from his shoulders, and a glittering H was stitched in gold thread upon his sleeve, and he was smiling up at them.

Lord Xin, the Heirmaster.

Cruelest of the Czar's War Council.

And Alexander's tutor.

(A NOTE ON THE WAR COUNCIL)

The Czar's War Council had five members in all. There was Ugor the Warmaster, who was strong; Pieter the Tallymaster, who was mathemagical; Blüstav the Alchemaster, who was useless and banished; Sir Klaus the Spymaster, who was [CLASSIFIED]; and Lord Xin the Heirmaster, who was cruel.

All of their jobs revolved around the Czar's ceaseless appetite for conquering. It was Ugor's job to lead the armies off to battle; Pieter's job to make sure they had enough swords and bullets; Blüstav's job to magic up enough silver to pay for it all; Sir Klaus's job to make sure the battle wasn't actually an ambush; and finally it was Lord Xin's job to make sure the next ruler of Petrossia was just as vicious and bloodthirsty as his father.

Apart from Alchemaster Blüstav, who had managed to turn himself into a pile of coins, no member of the War Council was doing worse at their job than Lord Xin. Alexander was proving to be a hopeless conqueror and a dreadful pupil. He had no butchery. No bloodthirst.

Instead, there was a stubborn streak of *kindness* in him.[9]

Lord Xin had tried his best to nurture his pupil's appetite for violence. Alexander had a whole *bedroom* full of crossbows. And yet, to this day, the prince hadn't murdered anyone. Not even accidentally.

The Heirmaster was beginning to get worried. Not just for the Empire's future, but for his own as well. If Alexander didn't start showing *some* improvement—perhaps by tormenting Bloodbath, for example, or bullying that wimp of a Tallymaster, or even just refusing to say please and thank you—then Lord Xin might find himself banished too, like Alchemaster Blüstav had been.

Which is why, when the Heirmaster strode into the kitchens, looking for his pupil, and spotted the prince playing hide-and-seek on the shelf with two forbidden friends, Lord Xin began to smile.

It was time to teach Alexander a lesson he would not forget.

---

9. One hot day in Swoon last year, the Heirmaster had even discovered Alexander putting sombreros on the severed heads spiked atop the palace gates—to stop them from getting sunburn.

6

The Heirmaster's Lesson

Reaching down, Lord Xin took the slender silver pipe that swung from his belt like a sword. It was not a flute but a flyte, an instrument that gave anyone skilled enough to play it the ability to fly.

Raising the flyte to his lips, Lord Xin trilled a low rising note. His feet rose up off the flagstones, above the stoves, toward the shelves. The din of the kitchen died down to almost silence as the cooks and maids stopped to gawp up at him. They quickly turned away and resumed their work again, though. It was not wise to stare too long at a member of the War Council.

On the shelf, Pieter shoved his hands into his pockets so Lord Xin wouldn't see them trembling. He tried to calm himself down using his usual method: first, he gave his fear a number roughly equivalent to how scared he was (at the moment, he was around five hundred and sixty-three thousand and eight times more afraid than usual), then found the number's square root, and kept going until his fear reached almost zero.

We'll be fine, he told himself, while Lord Xin's flyte got louder and nearer. *Alexander knows what to say. He got lost while playing, and we're helping him get back upstairs.*

The song trilled, closer and closer. Lord Xin stepped over the air as the musical notes stepped up and down their stave. He stopped playing, and fell down onto the windowsill beside them as lightly as a panther.

"Young Majesty," he said to Alexander, clipping his flyte back on his belt. "You're late for lessons. We were going to learn how the Czar kidnapped the Duke of Madri's poodle."[10]

"I got lost, Lord Xin," Alexander blurted out, eyes darting around. "I was playing sieges, and I charged down here, and Pieter and Teresa were helping me get back upstairs to the Royal Chambers, and they're not my best friends either so you can't chop off their heads because we didn't even eat any birthday cake."

It took every ounce of control Pieter had not to groan and slap his palm against his forehead. Opposite him, he saw Teresa's shoulders sag ever so slightly. Even Lord Xin looked disappointed. He gave a despairing sigh and rolled his eyes.

---

10. Dog biscuits laced with snoozeweed, in case you were wondering.

"We practice lying for two hours a day," he said to Pieter and Teresa. "He's actually getting *worse*."

Pieter began to back away from the Heirmaster. Teresa did the same. Over by a crate of dry sliced bread, she mouthed the words, "We're toast."

"Don't hurt them, Lord Xin!" Alexander ran forward, eyes trembling with tears.

"Quiet!" Lord Xin's face twisted into a snarl. "This is to teach you a lesson, Young Majesty. Friends make you weak. Friends will *betray* you. So watch closely. I do this for your own good."

In an instant, Lord Xin's dagger, made from the curved claw of a roc, was in his hand. Alexander threw back his head and started to wail.

"Wait, Heirmaster!" Pieter held up his hands, trying to take control, trying to save them. He spoke in his sternest voice. "As a fellow member of the Czar's War Council, I remind you that you have no authority to harm us."

Lord Xin's laugh was high and fluttery like a love song. "Incorrect, Tallymaster. Only the Czar can decide if *you* die. But as for the Spice Monkey . . ."

In an instant, the Heirmaster's dagger was at Teresa's throat. Pieter did not even have time to cry out. Lord Xin moved faster than a blur . . .

. . . so did Teresa. Her hand flew from her pocket in a spray of black dust, and the Heirmaster stumbled back with a shriek, wiping ground peppercorns from his eyes. Hot tears of hate streamed down his cheeks.

Teresa turned to run, and jerked to a stop. Lord Xin had caught hold of her plait. Winding her hair round his wrist like a rope, he hoisted her up into the air. Teresa cried out, feet kicking six inches off the shelf—then suddenly Lord Xin was scrabbling at his face, howling. A blazing pip chili had been stuffed up each of his nostrils. The green stems curled out of his nose like tusks.

He hacked with his dagger—Pieter's heart skipped in his chest—but it was a wild slice, and Teresa fell back to the shelf again. Her long white plait had been sheared off just below her neck. It swung limply from Lord Xin's fist.

Crouching down, Teresa had just enough time to scatter a fistful of hazelnuts behind her as she rolled to safety. Lord Xin stabbed at her a second time. Stepping forward, he slipped on them, arms flailing, perilously close to the shelf edge.

Seizing a bread roll, stale and hard as a rock, Teresa hefted it once and threw.

Her aim was perfect.

Clonk!

With a howl, the Heirmaster teetered off the edge and

vanished. He let out a long, high-pitched scream that pierced Pieter's ears. It cut out suddenly. Far below, the kitchen went back to its hubbub of voices and pans.

Pieter waited for shrieks from the cooks, the shattering of dropped china, yells for guards. Nothing came. Perhaps they'd thought the scream was a whistling kettle. Perhaps the steamy air had hidden the body for a few moments. They had to escape before the guards were called.

He ran straight for Teresa. Alexander did too. Neither of them bothered to go to the edge and look down at the Heirmaster's body. They were seven shelves above the granite flagstones. You didn't need to be a mathemagical genius to know that Lord Xin wasn't coming back up after falling that far.

"Teresa!" he cried, head reeling, thoughts a jumble. "Are you hurt?"

Teresa touched her head gingerly and winced. "I've had better haircuts. He won't be getting a tip, that's for sure."

She gave them one of her looks (the one with the sideways head and the wry smile). But her hands were trembling, and Pieter could see how shaken she really was. That had been close. Too close. He could still see in his mind the sharp claw of Lord Xin's dagger at her throat. There were several million parallel universes now, in which *she* was the one lying dead on the ground. The thought made him feel faint.

Alexander's eyes were raw and shiny. He looked like he might burst into tears again. He threw himself forward, hugging her tightly. "I hate birthdays," he sniffed, voice muffled against her chest. "I thought you were going to die, like my mama."

"She will die a lot more slowly and painfully than the Czarina did," a voice hissed behind them.

They all whirled around to see Lord Xin, scarlet faced and sweating. He tugged the blazing pip chilies from his nostrils like they were tiny, fiery turnips. He sneezed a gout of sizzling snot onto the shelf.

Pieter blinked, thinking: *Impossible, you're dead, I heard you fall. . . .*

Then he saw the flyte in the Heirmaster's hand, and his brain worked out the truth: the high-pitched scream had been the sound of the musical note that stopped Lord Xin from falling.

"Stay where you are!" he hissed when Teresa took a step toward him.

This time it was not the roc dagger in his hand, but a singing pistol. Teresa froze, and Pieter went icy with terror. The singing pistol was an assassin's weapon. It came from Soy and was illegal in every other land on Earth. When the trigger was pulled, a tiny alchemical device inside the barrel changed the bang into the sound of a blackbird's song.

"Don't think I won't kill all of you." Lord Xin's face was bright red with the chili heat and shame, and his eyes were swimming with mad, scalding tears. "I'll do it, and no one will ever know it was me. The cooks didn't see me fall. Now they won't hear a thing. Empty your pockets of all those little tricks, girl. *Now.*"

He means it, Pieter thought. *He's so mad, he'd even shoot Alexander.*

Beside him, Teresa must have realized the same thing, because slowly, she began to unbutton each patchwork pocket and send herbs and spices tumbling from her grasp.

"Good," Lord Xin said, looking a little calmer. "Now come stand with me, Young Majesty."

Alexander looked up at Teresa, and she nodded. He went, lip quivering, while Teresa emptied out the last of her pockets. Snoozeweed, lemon myrtle, dried nettlesting . . . they all formed a little pile around her feet.

"Wipe your eyes," Lord Xin snapped, snatching Alexander by the scruff of his dressing gown. He aimed the singing pistol at Teresa's heart. "Stand in front of me. Here. I want you to watch this."

Pieter tried to square root his terror again, but this time it was just too enormous. The chances the three of them would survive the next few minutes were one in a million and getting astronomically smaller with each passing second.

"That pocket there too," snarled Lord Xin, pointing his singing pistol to the woolen ginger pocket on Teresa's thigh.

Pieter's fists clenched. He knew what Teresa kept in that pocket. A claw-shaped glass bottle, full of a ginger-colored sludge that moved as lazily as syrup.

Their secret alchemy.

The Catastrophica potion.

And suddenly Pieter had an idea. An idea that could save them all. It was their only hope. Their months of experimenting, of try and fail and try again, had all distilled down to this one moment.

"Lord Xin, wait!" he cried. "That bottle is special. Teresa is—"

"Pieter!" she hissed. "Shut it!"

But he couldn't. Not when this could save her life. "She's an *alchemist*, Lord Xin. An alchemist who might actually be able to do alchemy! Do you know how many of them I have listed upstairs in my tallychamber? None! They all blow themselves up, or change themselves into coins like Blüstav did. But not Teresa. She's a genius!"

"You're lying," Lord Xin said, his raw nostrils flaring.

"Alchemy is chaos. It cannot be controlled. It wears off too *quickly*. I remember old Blüstav. A week at most, then *poof*! The potion wears off, and the thing changes back."

"I'm better than Blüstav," said Teresa suddenly, glancing over to Pieter as if to say, *I know what you're planning*. "I made this potion to last for years."

"Impossible!" Lord Xin snarled.

"Maybe even decades," said Teresa, unstoppering the bottle of Catastrophica with her thumb. "Let me prove it to you."

Pieter's heart was slamming in his chest. In all their tests so far, the potion had been completely unpredictable. Perhaps this latest version would work. Or maybe it would just explode, like most of their other attempts.

Either way, his brain pointed out, *it will deal with Lord Xin.*

Hiding his fear, Pieter leaned forward and raised his eyebrows persuasively at him. "A new Alchemaster! Just think how you'll be rewarded if you bring her to the Czar."

The Heirmaster's lust for reward fought with his thirst for revenge.

"Go on," said Teresa, holding up the bottle. "Pick something for me to change."

Lord Xin glanced around the shelf. The barrel of his singing pistol lowered for just a moment.

Teresa leaped forward, Catastrophica in hand.

(A NOTE ON *WHAT IF*)

If Teresa had been a little closer—

If her grip on the potion had been a little tighter—

If the hazelnut she slipped on had been a little smaller—

If Lord Xin had been a little slower—

If Alexander had been a little to the left—

Then this would be a very different story.

But this isn't a tale of *What If*.

This is the tale of *What Was*.

7

Alexander Turns Furry

The catastrophe unfolded in dreadful slow motion. Pieter saw everything with awful clarity—but was unable to move fast enough to stop it from happening. Lord Xin brought the singing pistol up, and he was too fast, and Teresa was too slow, and the barrel was aiming straight at her heart.

But then Teresa trod on one of the hazelnuts she had scattered over the shelf a few minutes beforehand, and went sprawling head over heels.

Pieter's ears filled with a chorus of birdsong, and behind Teresa something swift and deadly tore itself through the mint leaves and buried itself into the brick wall with a flash of blue sparks. It was only later on, when he saw the singing pistol's smoking barrel, that Pieter realized Teresa had just accidentally dodged a bullet.

At the time, he was too preoccupied watching the bottle

of Catastrophica to think about anything else.

It tumbled from her grasp as Teresa fell, spinning lazily, end over end, sending fat swirls of ginger potion sloshing into the air.

Towards Lord Xin, who ducked.

And Prince Alexander, who didn't.

There was a wet splatting sound, followed by a moment of stillness, broken only by the steady drip of ginger sludge from Alexander's hair, chin, ears, and hands. Crouched behind him, Lord Xin was completely dry. Only the barrel of his singing pistol was wet with the potion. The prince had been his barricade.

Teresa staggered to her feet, her expression slack with horror.

"Alexander!" she cried. *"Get the Catastrophica off you!"*

"The whaty-whatica?" said Alexander. He stood there in a puddle of potion. It glooped and slopped down his whole body in long syrupy strands.

"Holy Sohcahtoa," Pieter breathed.

"Is it bad if I swallowed some?" Alexander said with a gulp. "It wasn't mustard, was it? I'm allergic to mustard."

Pieter and Teresa and Lord Xin all backed away from the Prince of Petrossia with a kind of horrified fascination. But the moments passed, and Alexander didn't change.

There was no magical transformation. Luckily, there was no explosion, either. Alexander was still the same little boy, sitting in his dressing gown, his ginger hair unbrushed.

"Wait a second," Pieter said to Alexander. "You don't have *ginger* hair!"

Beside him, Teresa let out a little gasp that was equal parts horror and triumph. "He does now," she said.

Alexander tilted his head. "What do I have meow?" he said, then giggled. "I mean, what do I have *now*?"

That was how it began.

Pieter and Teresa's alchemy *did* work. It was just taking its time, because cats are lazy and stubborn creatures, and any potion that changes you into one will do so exactly when and as it pleases.

Pieter sniffed. There was a smell of burning. It was getting stronger. He cried out—*wisps of orange smoke were wafting out of the prince's ears!*

Now his nose!

Now a long twisting tendril curled from his behind like a tail!

Alexander hopped and crouched over the shelf. "What's happening?" he said, more confused than afraid. "I feel like I'm full of fizzy juice!"

With a blink, his pupils flattened from circles to slits.

Fur spiked up from his skin. Orange sparks jumped and fizzed, whizzing off his body and popping in puffs of pale pink smoke. It was as if he had fleas, and they had decided to set off a display of miniature fireworks.

Lord Xin backed away, staring at Prince Alexander, then at the singing pistol in his hand. The barrel had transformed into a long, curling tabby cat's tail. "Alchemy!" he cried. "Actual *alchemy*! What are the odds?"

There was a sucking sound. Alexander was starting to shrink. His dressing gown fell down on top of him like a collapsed circus tent. Out of the sleeve walked a very tiny, very ginger, and very soggy kitten.

Pieter and Teresa looked down at their friend—Alexander, Prince of Petrossia, Only Son of the Czar, Heir to the Iron Crown.

"Meow?" he said to them.

PART TWO

Gargantua

Words were originally magic, and even today retain much of their old magical power.

—SIGMUND FREUD

I shall now become a lion.

—*PUSS IN BOOTS*, CHARLES PERRAULT

1

The War Council Gathers

After Lord Xin summoned the guards—

After Pieter and Teresa were clapped in chains—

After they were thrown in the dungeons—

After Alexander ran away and hid in the herb garden—

After he was chased back out again by a rat, which bit his tail and gave him fleas—

After the cooks carefully sloshed the shelf clean of Catastrophica—

After it glugged down the drain, burping ginger-colored bubbles—

After it sluiced into the sewers, and then into the River Ossia—

After a group of carp swallowed it in much diluted form, and turned into the first catfish—

After all this happened, the Czar sat in his throne room, ready to admit defeat for the first time in his life.

It was a terrible feeling. It filled his head with gloom and his heart with bitterness, and he sat on his throne with an ashen face and a molten temper, trying to think of an answer to his problem:

How could his son become a conqueror now?

The question was an enemy more powerful and dangerous than any the Czar had fought before. He was no fool—mighty as he was, he knew that a day would come when old age would summon the Pale Traveler to take him to the land of the dead. What would happen to Petrossia then, with a cat for a king? The mighty empire he had built would crumble away to nothing.

He looked at the red velvet pillow down at his feet. Bloodbath had been banished to the hallway. Lounging on the pillow now was a little pile of ginger fur. Prince Alexander was contentedly pawing at a toy mouse.

"This is your fault," he growled at his son. "You were supposed to shoot *arrows* at the serfs, not make *friends* with them! How many crossbows does a lad have to get for his birthday? Where's your butchery? Where's your bloodthirst?"

Alexander dipped his little head. He held up his paw, and out slid five puny claws the size of nail clippings.

"Meow?" he said, swiping them back and forth.

The Czar made a *pff* sound. "What will you do with *them*? Scratch someone to death?"

Alexander did his best pounce on the toy mouse he had been playing with.

"Is that supposed to impress me?" The Czar shook his head. "I conquered the mice of Petrossia years ago. Some of them even serve me as soldiers. The Mousketeers would make ginger fur coats out of you. I doubt you could even defeat Bloodbath."

Alexander did not make a sound. He curled up very small on his cushion and looked up at his father, shame glittering in his green eyes.

The Czar stood up from his throne, pacing and seething. This problem was too daunting for him to face on his own. To defeat it, he would need to call upon the strength of his greatest warriors.

It was time to assemble the War Council.

They gathered in the Hall of Faces, the enormous gallery that sits at the center of the Winter Palace, where the four walls and most of the ceiling are covered by royal portraits.

From their gilded picture frames, the past kings of Petrossia glare in their thousands. Most are so ancient, so paint flaked and faded, it is like the hall is filled with rows of staring ghosts. They all look like the Czar: stern, with green eyes, and thick beards or mustaches. They have names like Vladimir the Savage, or Boris of the Nine Wives.[11]

It is always sunset in the Hall of Faces, no matter what the time of day. This is because, over the centuries, the portraits have slowly covered up all the windows. Now the only light comes from the tall doors at either end. Each is made of stained glass, and depicts a different battle the Czar has fought. *Total annihilation* is probably a more accurate description than *battle*. Red is the primary color.

It was in that emergency-colored light that the Czar stood looking at each of his War Council in turn.

"Warmaster Ugor, Heirmaster Xin, Spymaster Klaus," the Czar began. "I gather you here because I am fighting an unwinnable war and I am close to surrender. Never before have I battled so hard and so hopelessly against my enemy. Here he is: the future ruler of my empire."

In his hands was the red velvet pillow. The prince was on it, snoozing.

"Sire," said Lord Xin. "This kitten cannot rule Petrossia. You must adopt a *new* son."

---

11. Women rulers are forbidden in Petrossia. That helps explain why the country is in such a mess. You will not see any queens in the Hall of Faces—at least, not at first glance. Look closer, though, at the portrait of King Tiffany the Blood-drinker, and you will see a red-lipped gentleman, with what looks suspiciously like a squirrel's tail glued to his top lip.

"No adoption," grunted Ugor. He gestured with one enormous hand to the Hall of Faces. "The bloodline. Heirs must have royal ancestry."

Lord Xin shook his head. "But His Majesty had the entire royal family executed when He was crowned."

"A coronation to remember," said the Czar fondly.

"Yes, Your Majesty," said Lord Xin. "It was very generous of you to carry out the beheadings personally."

"Great-aunt Anastasia deserved nothing less." The Czar's wistful expression vanished. "Happy as that day was, it does now mean that Prince Alexander *will* one day inherit the throne of Petrossia. There is no one else. We must make him a conqueror before that happens. I ask you now: Do any of you know how to turn my son—this kitten—into a conqueror?"

Silence in the Hall of Faces.

"You are as much use as these portraits!" growled the Czar. He looked at his ancestors, purse lipped and silent. "Has my mighty and cunning War Council really been beaten by a kitten?"

Ugor scratched his scars and sucked his broken teeth. He was strong: the only person in the world who had managed a draw with the Czar in a thumb war. But how could his strength solve a problem like this?

As for Lord Xin, he spoke seven languages; he knew poisons that could kill quickly, or painfully, or silently; he could teach sword skills and siege tactics. Yet what good was all his knowledge and cunning, when he did not know alchemy?

And Sir Klaus the Spymaster, who sat through the discussion too, remained hidden from everyone but the Czar. He could conceal himself in the smallest shadow and vanish like smoke through a crack in the wall. But what use were his skills now?

"Forgive us, Majesty," Lord Xin said, bowing low. "We are soldiers, not potion makers."

At that, the Czar stroked his mustache. The Heirmaster's words had given him a thought. Perhaps things were not hopeless after all. "You are right, Lord Xin," he said at last. "Warriors and tutors and spies cannot solve this problem for me—only an *alchemist* can."

Lord Xin frowned. "But Alchemaster Blüstav is banished," he said. "And possibly still made of money."[12]

"I wasn't talking about *that* old fraud," said the Czar. "I wasn't talking about *him* at all."

12. Actually, Blüstav's alchemy had already worn off. He changed back into a man whilst piled up in the Duke of Madri's treasure chamber, and escaped with several priceless alchemical books. A letter from the Duke was already heading for Petrossia, demanding compensation—and a refund of that siege cannon.

2

The Gigantic Idea

Pieter and Teresa were dragged up from the dungeons and plonked in front of the Czar. They were both so wrapped up in lead chains they looked like fat mounds of gray spaghetti, each with a little meatball head on top. The afternoon light shining through the stained-glass doors was the color of massacres. It suited the Czar's expression perfectly.

"Think very carefully about what you say from now on," he said to the two of them. "Because I have a sword, and you're chained up, and I'm in a head-chopping mood. The only reason you're alive at all is because of *this*."

With one hand, he snatched up Alexander by the scruff of the neck and tossed him forward. The fluffy prince flew through the air with a yowl. Landing on his feet, he ran up Teresa's chains and cuddled against her cheek.

"Alexander!" she cried. "I'm so sorry for mixing you up in this."

But the prince just licked her nose, then looked over at Pieter and purred.

"He's forgiven them already?" The Czar shook his head in disbelief. "Lord Xin, haven't you taught him to hold a *grudge*?"

"Many, many times," said the Heirmaster with a pained sigh. "Too much of his mother in him."

"You leave Alexander alone!" yelled Teresa, face red and furious. "And his mama too!"

"Hold your tongue, Spice Monkey!" Lord Xin roared.

Teresa stuck it out at him. "Why should I?"

The Czar raised one slanted eyebrow, as if it were a guillotine.

Pieter's jaw dropped, like a head into a basket. "Oh no," he whispered. Teresa was done for now. *Why should I?* was one of those questions—along with *May I have a holiday?* and *Is there any pudding?*—that serfs were forbidden to ask. The Czar never bothered to answer. He let his sword do the talking, and its reply was always short, sharp, and to the point.

There was a metallic scraping sound that ended in a high ringing hum as the Czar drew his blade from its scabbard. The sword glinted in the bloody light of the hall. Its name was Viktor, because it had never belonged to a Loser.

"Viktor?" said the Czar to his blade. "Cut this insolent serf down to size."

"Wait, Majesty!" Ugor lumbered forward and murmured in the Czar's ear.

The Czar's teeth made the sound of breaking bones as he ground them together. "Ugor is right," he muttered. "We need her."

"Killing her is out of the question," said Lord Xin into his other ear. "Agonizing torment, on the other hand . . ."

The Czar gave an evil chuckle. "War Council, you advise me well." And looking straight at Teresa, he sentenced her to the most gruesome torture he could think of.

(It involved a teaspoon and two barrels of beetroot soup.)

"Go tell the cooks!" the Czar ordered Ugor.

"And make sure they go easy on the seasoning," said Teresa as he left.

This only made the Czar angrier, and so Teresa's torture was made even more painful.

(It now also involved two hungry piranhas in a pair of water-filled rain boots.)

"Prepare the rubber boots, Lord Xin! And make sure they're a snug fit."

"Gladly, Your Majesty," said the Heirmaster.

Pieter struggled and yelled, but his shackles were wrapped

around him too tight. All he could do was watch as Lord Xin tipped Teresa over in her chains, and began to roll her like a barrel out the door.

"Teresa!" Pieter cried, twisting his neck. "I'll save you! I'll do whatever it takes!"

He tried to sound brave. He tried to sound certain. He was roughly thirty percent successful. In any exam hall in Eureka, that was a fail.

Teresa didn't say anything. She just gave Pieter a look he had never seen before: a trembling look, full of longing for *What If*, and regret for *What Was*.

Alexander gave a hiss and pounced for Lord Xin's shin, shredding the silk trouser leg with his claws. But the Heirmaster just shook him off, and the prince went rolling across the floor, mewling for his best friend.

It was all down to Pieter now.

All around him, the portraits glared down, making him prickle and sweat. He shut his eyes, trying to think. Long reams of mathemagical symbols scribbled across the blackboards of his eyelids. If only he could join them together into a great formula that would somehow work out a way to survive . . . But the only thing that kept coming into his mind were the words of the Czar.

Cut this insolent serf down to size.

"There is a way you can save the Spice Monkey," said the Czar, pulling Pieter from his thoughts. "Do you know what it is?"

Pieter made a kind of strangled whimper. It was the noise he used to make back in the exam halls of Eureka, whenever he needed more time.

"Don't panic," said the Czar. His voice was almost kindly. "I'll tell you." His finger, thick as a musket barrel, pointed down at Prince Alexander. "Change. My. Son."

Pieter's dread became relief. He didn't need to come up with a plan—the Czar had given one to him!

"Yes, Your Majesty!" he cried. "I promise! Teresa and I will not rest until we find a way to turn Alexander back to a boy. Will you bring her back now? Please don't hurt her."

(It was probably not a good time for Pieter to tell the Czar that he had no idea how they would do this. Teresa had made the Catastrophica ten thousand times more potent than Blüstav's weak potions—it wasn't like they could just wait for it to wear off. And just how did you reverse alchemy anyway?)

"Oh no, Tallymaster," said the Czar softly, interrupting Pieter's thoughts. "You mistake me. Why would I want Alexander back to the way he was? I want you to change him into something else entirely. I want you to make him a *conqueror.* You see, I need an heir who'll appreciate all the crossbows I've been giving him. I had hoped Lord Xin might teach the boy a bit of bloodthirst. But now that I have an Alchemaster, I can just change Alexander to become exactly the sort of son I want. Surely there's a potion that will turn his kindness into cruelty?"

Just like that, Pieter's relief turned back to dread. Giving Alexander paws, claws, and a tail had been terrible enough—but that was all *outside* changes, and accidental too. Under all that ginger fur, he was still a little boy who liked birthday cake, and missed his mother. He was still their friend.

But changing him *inside* . . .

Turning him *cruel* . . .

And doing it not by accident but *on purpose* . . .

Pieter shuddered. Then he wouldn't be Alexander anymore, would he? How could he do that to their friend? And yet it was the only way to save Teresa (and probably himself) from long and terrible torture, topped off with a short sharp chop.

Again, he tried to think of his own solution.

Again, he heard the Czar's voice in his head, like an endless echo.

Cut this insolent serf down to size . . .

Down to size . . .

Size . . .

"THAT'S IT!" Pieter shouted. "I'LL DO IT! I'LL MAKE ALEXANDER INTO A CONQUEROR!"

The Czar's words—*Cut this insolent serf down to size*—had struck him like a bolt of inspiration, and sparked an idea in his head. His mind was thrumming with the wonder of it. His goose bumps prickled with its simple mathemagical elegance. It was so stunning, so staggering, so truly spectacular that his own brain could barely conceive of its consequences.

The Czar gave an eager smile. "Good, Tallymaster. Tell me how."

"What we'll do is—" Pieter stopped himself just in time. He was so excited, he had almost forgotten to do the smart thing.

Instead of explaining, Pieter just gave the Czar his best attempt at one of Teresa's looks (the one with the raised eyebrows and the smugness).

"First, send for Ugor and Lord Xin," he said. "Tell them not to hurt Teresa."

The Czar looked peeved. He was not used to being given orders. But eventually, he looked over Pieter's shoulder and said, "Sir Klaus? Do as the Tallymaster says."

Suddenly, Pieter became aware of a presence behind him, standing right on the spot where he could not turn his head.

The Spymaster had been here in the hall all along, listening but unseen. There was the barest flicker of movement, the smallest swish of sound, and Sir Klaus was gone. The strangest thing of all was that Pieter was sure the doors had neither opened nor closed.

The Czar held up his hands—a gesture he was not used to making.

"Happy?" he said.

Pieter nodded.

"Good." The Czar folded his arms. "Explain. And be convincing. For the Spice Monkey's sake."

Pieter took a deep breath, wondering where to start.

"The truth is," he began, "Alexander is going to be a cat for a long, long time. The Catastrophica won't wear off, like Blüstav's alchemy. Not for years. Maybe even decades. And I don't know if anyone can change that.

"But just because Alexander is a cat," he continued hurriedly, seeing the Czar's hand start to stray toward Viktor, "doesn't mean he can't be a conqueror. After all, isn't the Lion the King of the Beasts?"

The Czar scowled, as if this was all some joke, and he'd already guessed the punchline and didn't find it funny. "Alexander isn't anything like a lion, Tallymaster. He's tiny."

Pieter didn't say anything to that. He just did Teresa's

trick of raising the eyebrows, and waiting. He square-rooted his fear while the seconds passed.

To the Czar's credit, it didn't take long for him to figure it out.

"A *growth* potion," he growled.

"Exactly, Your Majesty. *'Cut this insolent serf down to size,'* you said. Size is the solution. It's like a multiplication problem . . . How do you get the answer? Make the number *bigger.* We can make him so enormous, he'll be undefeatable. But I have to be with Teresa. We're a team. We can only do alchemy together."

"Hmm." The Czar stroked his mustache as he considered Pieter's plan. He paced down the hallway, looking at his ancestors. At their beards, plaited with knucklebones. At their eyes the color of greed. At their iron stares and steely smiles and clenched fists.

Then he looked at his son, who was prancing about, playing with the cushion tassels.

"You have until the last day of Dismember," he said to Pieter.

"The last day of Dismember?" Pieter spluttered. "But that's less than two weeks away! The Catastrophica took us all of Bloom, Swoon, and Sway to make."

"Then you best get to the Winter Palace laboratory quickly."

Behind Pieter, the doors burst back open. Lord Xin came back in, rolling a chained-up Teresa with barely suppressed fury. Craning his neck around, Pieter was relieved to see no beetroot soup stains dribbled down her chin. He quickly counted her toes. She still had all ten. It looked like he'd saved her before the torture could start.

"You could have waited until the piranhas had had a *little* nibble . . . ," Lord Xin complained.

The Czar waved him away impatiently. "I am giving the alchemists a chance."

"What's going on?" Teresa looked bewildered as Ugor tore off her chains. "I thought I was getting tortured?"

"Change of plan," said the Czar. "You're being promoted. Welcome to the War Council."

The butler came in, carrying a neatly folded red velvet robe. He draped it over Teresa's shoulders. Stitched in gold thread below the hood was the letter A.

Pieter had seen the robe before. It was Blüstav's old Alchemaster's uniform.

Teresa gave Pieter one of her looks. The one with the bewilderment rapidly turning to rage.

"Pieter Abadabacus," she growled, her voice scarily similar to the Czar's. "What. Have. You. Done?"

(A NOTE ON GOSSIP)

It is generally considered that Light is the fastest thing there is, but that is only true over long distances. When it comes to short sprints, Gossip is far quicker. That is why—way before anyone in Petrossia had even seen the prince for themselves—children skipping in the school yards were already singing rhymes about what had happened:

"Teresa! Teresa! Can you believe her?
Brewed a disaster with her best friend Pieter!
Got herself a notion to make a special potion,
Went and caused one very furry commotion!
Got a big promotion for causing this calamity,
Now they do alchemy for the royal family!
Catastrophe! Catastrophe! Emphasis on cat!
What can the alchemists do to fix that?"

It was a more or less accurate report of events, except for one thing: Pieter and Teresa were most definitely not best friends.

3

Pieter Dodges a Flying Library

"You are worse than stinksheep's wool!" Teresa bellowed. "More disgusting than a puspig's trotters! More horrible than a bilebear's burps!"[13]

Pieter flinched. Teresa's insults hurt, but they were not nearly as painful (or blunt) as the alchemy books she had been hurling at him when they had first been locked inside the Winter Palace's laboratory.

The laboratory was at the very top of the North Spire. Despite being half destroyed by its previous owner, it was still much larger than where they'd made the Catastrophica potion. The walls were lined with shelves gone bow-middled with books: recipe collections, theoretical tomes, leather-bound diaries of ancient Alchemasters. . . . There was a nearly endless supply for Teresa to chuck at Pieter's head.

---

13. For more information on the unpleasant animals of Petrossia, see Professor Fauna's Odious Encyclopedia: a list of all things fetid and foul. Be sure to handle the pages with rubber gloves.

Her aiming ability was roughly twice as good as Pieter's ducking ability. Pieter had been able to read some of the titles as they'd flown toward his face. Ovid's *Metamorphosis*, Dorn's *Philosophia Speculativa*, *Libra Gargantua* by Grimaldi the Most Wise . . . That one had been particularly painful.

Apart from the books that were now splayed all over the floor, the only other things in the laboratory were a fireplace (gone out), a cauldron (rusted), a mouse (white), spiders (enormous), and a squiggle of strangely shaped glass tubes all connected on a worktop. Attached together, they looked like very neat joined-up handwriting, spelling a long nonsense word across the table.

"Because of you," Teresa raged, "we're helping a vicious, murderous bully turn his innocent son into a gigantic monster!"

"Stop yelling at me!" Pieter yelled back.

Teresa obliged him by throwing the lab equipment at him instead. He ducked behind the cauldron as glass tubes shattered on the shelves above his head like clear crystal fireworks, sending shards tinkling to the floor.

"What was I supposed to do?" he yelled over all the smashing. "I thought it was the smart choice!"

Teresa, holding a Q-shaped alembic in her hands, paused. "But not the *right* one," she said.

Pieter frowned. Teresa wasn't making any sense. "If a choice is smart, of course it's going to be right," he explained to her. "Only *stupid* choices are wrong."

"Ugh!" The bulb of glass in her hands flew toward him like a cannonball. "How can a genius be so *idiotic*?!"

Pieter threw himself into the rusted cauldron for protection. He toppled in headfirst and curled up at the bottom.

"I ought to light the fireplace and boil you in that thing!" Teresa seethed.

Pieter double-checked with his brain that she was only joking. There was an alarmingly high probability that she wasn't.

"Oh, what's the point?" he heard her say. "Everything's turned out wrong. Operation: *His Royal Whiskers* was a total failure . . . and all because I tripped on a hazelnut."

"Operation: *His Royal Whatnow*?" Pieter asked, risking a peek out of the cauldron.

Teresa looked ready to hurl some more insults or large objects at him. But gradually her anger drained away, until she just looked ashen faced and beaten.

"Operation: *His Royal Whiskers*," she said, sliding to the floor and hugging her knees. "The secret plan I had. The one I didn't tell you about. The real reason I made the Catastrophica potion. You see, I'm a traitor."

Pieter shook his head uneasily. His eyes flicked around the room, wondering if the Spymaster was listening. "You mustn't say that," he said to her. "It was all an accident. You never meant to use the Catastrophica on Alexander *on purpose* . . . did you?"

"Of course not," said Teresa, head in her hands. "I meant to use it on the *Czar*."

(A NOTE ON TRAITORS)

Somewhere in Pieter's tallychamber, there was a list entitled *Traitors to the Czar.*

It had nothing written on it but the title.

Because there weren't any.

It wasn't that traitors didn't exist—it was more that they didn't exist long enough for Pieter to count them up and jot down their names.

This was all because of the Czar's Spymaster. Never in the history of Petrossia had there been such a skilled and mysterious infiltrator as Sir Klaus. He uncovered every plot before it could happen; exposed every assassin before they could strike; seized every bribe before it could tempt.

Not even the War Council knew what he looked like. It was rumored that he was a Vizard—a master of disguise, able to wear different faces as if they were masks. It was because of Sir Klaus that the list of traitors was always blank, and the spikes on the Winter Palace walls were always occupied.

But no longer. Pieter's list needed updating. The

gatehouse needed another couple of severed heads.

Teresa Gust—Petrossia's new Royal Alchemaster—was a secret traitor.

And Pieter Abadabacus was her unwitting coconspirator.

How long would it take for Sir Klaus to discover them?

4

Operation: His Royal Whiskers (Parts One and Two)

Pieter remembered the day in Eureka, just before the Czar had come, when his tutors had taught him that there were numbers *below* zero. Minus one, minus two, minus three, and so on—all the way to minus infinity. That same day, Pieter had learned that far below his feet, on the other side of the Earth, people on the fifth continent might be walking upside down. It was a very disorienting day.

Now he felt the same dizziness—the same reeling feeling that his whole world had just shifted. A secret lay beneath everything Teresa had ever told him. And its name was Operation: *His Royal Whiskers.*

He tumbled out of the cauldron and tiptoed across the broken glass as fast as he could, until he could yank Teresa close enough to hiss furiously in her ear, "The Spymaster is going to have our heads for this!"

"That's why I didn't tell you," she said back. "If the plan got discovered, you couldn't be accused of treason. Just stupidity."

"I thought we were trying to get rid of the kitchen's rats!"

"The Czar's a far bigger menace than rats, Pieter. If I'd managed to change him into a sweet little kitten, the conquering would stop. And Bloodbath could get revenge: I hate the way that poor poodle is always getting kicked around."

"You lied to me. You used me!"

"What did you expect? I kidnapped you in the middle of the night!"

"But I thought we were friends."

"We are! Friends are the only thing that can stand up to a bully."

"You don't stand up to bullies, Teresa! You survive them, until eventually they leave you alone. That's the smart choice."

Anger flashed across her face like thunder. She went to the window and tore open the curtains. Her finger jabbed against the glass. "Not everyone survives, Pieter."

He looked to where she pointed: beyond the courtyard, just short of the gatehouse towers.

The Winter Palace graveyard.

Old serfs and soldiers, buried in row upon row upon row. And in the middle of them all was the Chapel of the Frozen Tear, carved out of an iceberg that had been dragged from the river, where the Czar's beloved czarina lay in her coffin of ice and ether.

"Not everyone survives," Teresa said again, her eyes glittering like evening stars, and Pieter knew she was right. Many, many times over.

"Now do you see why I'm a traitor? Now do you see why I can't turn Alexander into an unstoppable furry . . ." Teresa trailed off. Her eyes went wide and her jaw dropped.

Pieter gulped. He knew that look: knew it very well, and right now he feared it very much.

"Oh no," he said. "You've had an idea, haven't you?"

Teresa gave a cryptic smile. "No," she said, "I've just reconsidered *your* idea. Maybe it isn't so terrible after all. What if we really *did* turn Alexander enormous? What if we made him into an unconquerable furry war machine?"

A bewildered Pieter rubbed the bumps on his head. "But when *I* suggested that, you threw books at my head for an hour."

"That was to knock some sense into you," Teresa said with a wave of her hand. "Now I've changed my mind."

"Why?"

"I'm an alchemist," she said. "What do you expect? Listen, Pieter: if we only change Alexander on the *outside*, he'll still be our friend on the inside. Think about it—*what if we make Alexander big enough to conquer the Czar himself?*"

Pieter's hands flew up to his ears, but there was no way to unhear those words. Now he was a traitor no matter what.

If he helped Teresa, that was treason. If he did nothing, while she went ahead with her plan, that was treason too.

"Oh no," he groaned.

"Alexander could take over the throne," Teresa said, pacing around the lab and getting more and more excited. "He could replace the Czar and become Emperor—no, wait—Em*purrer*. Free the serfs, stop the conquering, declare peace . . . And once the Czar is safely locked down in his own dungeon, we can work on reversing all the alchemy, so Alexander doesn't have to wait years until he changes back to a boy. . . ." She clapped her hands together. "It's perfect!"

"It's *suicide*," Pieter corrected.

Anger flashed in her voice like thunder. "No, it's standing up to a bully."

Pieter threw up his hands and pulled at his hair. "The bully is an eight-foot-tall killing machine!! And you're twelve!"

"Twelve and a bit," she said with a scowl.

"He has a suit made of titanium armor," Pieter huffed, counting reasons off on his fingers. "Your suit is mostly made of pockets."

Teresa looked down at all her patchwork pouches. "They're full of surprises, though."

"He's got a hundred armies! A War Council! A sword!"

There in the laboratory, Teresa turned to look at him: starlit eyes like supernovas. "And who have I got?" she asked.

She stared at him.

And stared.

And didn't stop staring.

Pieter covered his face with his hands and groaned. He didn't believe it. All she had to do was ask a *question* . . .

"Just promise me you won't get me guillotined," he said through his fingers.

She nodded solemnly. "I promise that I will never personally guillotine you."

"I don't want to get my head chopped off, Teresa."

"I know."

"I *like* my head."

"I like your head too. It complements your shoulders perfectly."

"And no more fibs, either."

She nodded.

"And no more chucking heavy books at me."

She smiled. "Deal. From now on, I will only throw paperbacks."

"That's not what I—"

"I know what you meant, you silly grottygoat!" Her grin turned suddenly serious. "No more fibs. No more fighting. I promise, Pieter. And what about you? Are you part of Operation: *His Royal Whiskers*, or not?"

Mathemagically, it was still almost hopeless. It was still

a stupid mistake. But maybe there was another way to work out what was right and wrong. You used your heart instead of your head, and courage instead of cleverness. Pieter had never made a decision like this before. It felt like learning mathemagics all over again.

"Count me in," he said.

The days flew by in a blur. Ideas and experiments from morn to dusk. Cauldron bubble and boil and stir. Mix and mingle, pinch and sprinkle, stoke the fire and feed the flames. Sizzle and spark, spit and shout. *Too hot*—it's not—*it is, WATCH OUT!*

Every day at least one BOOM. Clear the smoke out of the room.

We're gonna need another cauldron. . . . This one melted, last one rusted, how many is it that we've busted? How many times now have we tried?

Doesn't matter. Trial and error. Try and try and try again. Fail again just like before. Each time fail a little less, and learn a little more.

Dismember's ending, autumn's going. Welkin's near and winter's coming. Just keep working, don't stop hoping. Count the days down: ten, nine, eight. *We still have time.* It's not too late.

Book stacks teeter on the table, rising up like towers.

Study, light a tinderfly. Long, slow, fruitless hours. Yawn and stretch. No time for sleep. Keep eyes open. *Got to keep* . . .

Snore and dream, head on page. Jerk awake. Shake Teresa. Look out at another sunrise. Wipe the sleep from tired eyes.

Today might be the day. Maybe. *Knock, knock*: the maids with toast and tea.

That was how it went.

The Great, Gigantic Experiment.

"I give up," Pieter said after their tenth try that day. "Until tomorrow, at least."

He heaved shut another book, leaned back in his chair and rubbed his eyes. It was eight of the eve. Another whole day of experimenting, and all they had learned was ever more imaginative ways to destroy a cauldron. Their latest one sat in a blackened lump by the door.

"I didn't think it was possible to set fire to metal," Teresa said, nudging the charred cauldron with her foot. "Oh well. At least we've learned something. Today hasn't been a total waste."

Pieter went and divided the curtains in two, then pulled up the sash to let out the burnt iron smell. The wind that came in was cold and spiteful. It pinched at his bare arms, raising goose bumps.

Teresa came over and wrapped a blanket around his shoulders. Together, they peered out from the North Spire, down at the world. Far off, the River Ossia wove a dark path to the sea and the glittering lights of Port Xanderberg. Pieter could see the first few icebergs drifting down the river from the glaciers to the north, like a pod of white whales. Looking at them sent shivers through him. Winter was almost here, and with it the end of the Czar's patience.

"We're running out of time," Teresa said quietly, pulling the window shut.

Pieter didn't answer. Anything he said would only make him worry more. He stared at their reflections in the glass. They looked like ghosts, dead and gone already.

Nothing they tried worked. He was honestly starting to wonder if they really could do alchemy. Maybe making the Catastrophica was just a fluke. Three days until the end of Dismember, and they were no closer to finding the recipe for a growth potion. Teresa had poured out endless ideas, but Pieter couldn't get a single one of them to actually *work*.

He tried counting things to keep from panicking. Two wings of the Winter Palace, their walls painted eggshell blue. Eight hundred windows, each fringed with white cornices, like icing on a cake. Eighty-seven statues in the Fountain of Sobs, weeping hundreds of tears a second. Six new heads, spiked on the gatehouse wall. Holy Sohcahtoa, counting hadn't calmed him down at all.

"Shouldn't our fairy folkmother appear about now?" he said with a shiver. "I'd even be happy if Rumpelstilzki showed up."

Teresa glanced sharply at one corner of the room. "I don't think my folkmother knows anything about alchemical theory."

Pieter bumped his head against the glass. "She could at least change our luck, though."

"Our luck's good," Teresa said in her sternest voice. "It's your head that's the problem, Pieter. You've got to think harder."

She didn't say it in a mean way, but her words still stung. They were best friends, through danger and disaster, and Pieter had vowed to help her even though it might cost him his life. He'd crossed his heart, spat on his palm, and sealed the handshake with the promise rhyme. *What's been spoken can't be broken: these thirteen words will be my token.*

"I'm trying my best—" he insisted, but Teresa gripped his shoulders and interrupted.

"*Most* of you is," she said, staring at him intently, like she was trying to peer into his head. "Ninety-nine percent of you. But over the last few days I've been realizing the truth more and more. There's still some part of you—the genius bit that thinks in sums and survival percentages—that won't help. And if we're to make this potion, that's the part of Pieter Abadabacus that I need most of all!"

Pieter opened his mouth to argue, but couldn't get any words out. At last, he just slumped his shoulders. Maybe Teresa was right. Maybe there was a tiny fraction of him—the most mathemagical bit of his brain—that still saw the fight against the Czar as a terrible mistake.

"Don't worry," Teresa said, shaking him from his thoughts. "There's a way to convince you—every single bit of you—that our plan and our potion is the right thing to do." She bit her lip. "But it'll be hard on you, Pieter. I wouldn't be your best friend if I didn't tell you that."

He raised his head. "And *I* wouldn't be *your* best friend if I didn't trust you," he said. "What is it, then? What will convince me?"

She furrowed her brow, started several times to explain, until finally she just said simply: "The truth."

Pieter scratched his head. "I don't understand."

Teresa gave a small smile and took a step backwards. "Then I'll let our fairy folkmother explain," she said.

That's when Pieter noticed the little old grandma in the corner.

5

Peekaboo from the Fairy Folkmother

Standing by the fireplace, utterly still, was the most camouflaged old granny Pieter had ever seen. She resembled nothing so much as a chameleon: boggly eyes, leathery skin, gnarled hands clutching her old broom as if it were a branch. Her dress and shawl were made from the Petrossian royal colors—emerald, iron, and sky blue—in the same pattern as the Winter Palace's wallpaper, making her blend in perfectly with the chimney-breast wall behind her.

"Holy Sohcahtoa!" Pieter breathed. How long had the old grandma been standing there? She'd just *appeared*, as if by magic.

"Pieter Abadabacus, meet our fairy folkmother: Amnabushka Baba Gale," Teresa said, introducing them. "I've known Amna for a long, long time."

Amnabushka gave a crooked little bow. "Tallymaster and me have met before, my Patra," she said.

With a jolt, Pieter realized that was true. He had seen Amnabushka before: not just once, but thousands of times. She was always up and down the palace corridors, brushing away dust with her old broom of birch. Almost every day, on his way to his tallychamber or War Council meetings,

Pieter had passed her by without a second glance. He tried to remember her entry in the Groansday book.

49: AMNABUSHKA, PALACE SWEEP.
Born in Tumber, conquered in the Western Woodn't.
Age: 89,801.

He'd always assumed that her age must have been an error or a joke. But suddenly, with a strange prickling feeling, he wondered if it was. *The wildfolk measure their age not in years but in the miles they have traveled*, Teresa had said. Could Amnabushka really be her fairy folkmother, like in *Cindestrella* and all the other stories? Why else would she appear, here and now at their hour of need?

"How did you get up here?" Pieter asked her.

"By broom," said Amnabushka, holding it out to him.

Pieter gave her a skeptical glance. "You *flew*?"

Amna gave a mad old laugh that ended in a sneeze. "Are we wildfolk nothing but simple fairy tale witches to you? No, my broom brought me here because dust gets everywhere—so because I am the Palace Sweep, I am allowed where I wish."

"The guards always let old Amna pass," Teresa explained. "She was the one who slipped the snoozeweed in the Czar's samovar on Alexander's birthday. And she was the one who was going to pour the Catastrophica down his snoring throat, before Operation: *His Royal Whiskers* went wrong."

"Guards just look right through me," Amna said. "Especially when I've got my peekaboo on."

Suddenly, she hummed, fluttered her fingers up and down her broom as if it were an oboe, and drew a hieroglyph in the air with her thumb.

And Pieter couldn't see her anymore.

It wasn't that she was *invisible*. Pieter knew she was still there. He just couldn't *notice* her. The first time he tried, he blinked, and realized he was actually staring at the fireplace instead. He rubbed his eyes, tried again, and got distracted by a bit of peeling wallpaper behind her.

Pieter grit his teeth and squinted, forcing himself not to look away from the spot where he knew Amnabushka stood. The old granny was like dust in his eyes. Pieter couldn't look at her for more than a moment before he had to wipe her away.

"She knows magic!" The realization was so sudden Pieter couldn't stop from blurting it out.

Wiping away the air with one hand, Amnabushka took off her peekaboo enchantment. "Babapatra only taught me the small spells," she said, and threw back her shawl.

Pieter breathed in sharply. Beneath her striped hood, Amnabushka Baba Gale had starry eyes and long white hair tied in a hundred braids. Swinging at the end of each one was a charm: little bells the shape of foxgloves, a marbled cat's eye, twine-tied sprigs of mintflower, a wooden ankh, a reindeer's tooth . . . and an iron wedding ring.

"You're not just one of the wildfolk," Pieter whispered. "You're one of the Baba Sisters."

Over the past few months, Pieter had tried to find out more about the roaming people, looking for some clue as to Teresa's origins. There were dozens of different wildfolk: some tracked the reindeer herds across the Waste; others took great vaulted circus tents from town to town; still more lived in colorful trundle wagons and kept quiet company with the trees.

None were quite like the Baba Sisters. It was said they began back in the reign of Boris of the Nine Wives, who had tried to force Babapatra, Queen of Eglyph, to marry him. She had escaped instead, and freed his nine brides too, and fled deep into the Western Woodn't with them to hide.

There, she taught them magic.[14]

---

14. Not particularly hard to do. Even those who do not believe in magic will know a little: for magic is only words, said or sung at the right time and in the right way. Only words, and nothing else. Why else do you think it is called a "spell?"

Here is an example: Have you noticed how the phrase "Would you like pudding?" has the amazing ability to make room in your belly for more food, when just ten seconds ago you were certain that even one more mouthful would be enough to make you burst? "Would you like pudding?" is a powerful magic spell, you see.

Others joined them—those widowed and wearied by the endless wars—and soon they were a gang of feared outlaws known as the Baba Sisters.

Every czar since Boris had sent soldiers into the trees, to track down their pyramid camps. The Baba Sisters had been hunted mercilessly. Over the years, the nine brides had been recaptured and enslaved one by one, until finally Babapatra was killed at the Battle of One Knee.

"Yes, a Baba Sister I was, many miles ago," said Amna, touching the iron ring charm in her hair. "And a bride of Boris before that. And a girl of Albion before that. Three lives I've lived, and three names. I was born as Abigail, and then I became Baba Gale, but now I am just old Amnabushka. A crone in the corner no one notices, gathering dust."

"But why?" Pieter said to Amna in wonder. "Why be a slave for so long? If you're some kind of witch, why don't you fly off on your broom? And why don't you take the Czar away with you, while you're at it, and drop him on an iceberg in the middle of the Boreal Sea?"

Amnabushka swung her head slowly to look at Teresa, her charms going *tinkle* and *chink*.

"I know, I know," Teresa said, rolling her eyes. "He sounds like an idiot when you first meet him. Give him a chance." She took Pieter's arm. "Of course Amna can't fly, Pieter.

Levitation is a powerful spell. It requires asking Gravity to temporarily forget about bringing you back to the ground—something it's not going to do unless it owes you a huge favor."

"And even then," Amna explained, "you must be very polite. Magic, after all, is simply an Asking. And an Asking is never granted if you do not say your please-and-thank-yous."

"Not even Babapatra knew a spell as big as flying," Teresa continued.

"If only she had," said Amna, sorrow glittering in her eyes. She stared out the window at the Fountain of Sobs, where the marble Queen of Eglyph stood still at the end of all her miles, and wept bitter tears of defeat. "Maybe then her soul would not have been sent away with the Pale Traveler at the Battle of One Knee, and maybe I would still be free."

Pieter tried not to feel disappointed in their fairy folk-mother. "So if you can't fly, what magic *can* you do?" he asked.

"Pieter!" Teresa nudged him and scowled. "Questioning a Baba Sister's magic is rude."

Amna straightened her crooked spine. "I know the whistle that brings forth a hovering light that leads you to something lost. I can charm a bell so that it chimes whenever it hears lies. I have my peekaboo."

Pieter tried his best to look impressed. It seemed like their fairy folkmother knew spells of traveling, and trickery, and disguise. Useful when hiding out in the Woodn't but not right now. They needed thunderbolts called from the sky. Swords imbued with holy power. Things like that.

In short, they needed a miracle.

"Can't you summon us an angel?" he asked. "Or shape-shift into a dragon? You couldn't by any chance make a little kitten grow enormous, could you?"

Teresa nudged him again, harder. "She *does* know a curse that'll make your eyebrows grow up your forehead until they reach your hair. Sort your manners out!"

"My spells are small," said Amna, hobbling up to him. "But still, perhaps, I can help. It is you and my Patra Teresa who hold the power to defeat the Czar—it is within your minds. But part of *your* mind is locked, Pieter. Maybe I can provide the key."

Leaning forward, Amnabushka touched her glass cat's eye charm and sighed across the laboratory windowpane.

"This is the spell for homesickness," she said, drawing a hieroglyph on the glass. "The spell that shows you where you are from."

Pieter frowned. "What good will seeing my tally-chamber . . ."

The words died in his throat. The window was changing, like a magic mirror in a fairy tale. Outside, the Winter Palace and the world beyond it could still be dimly seen—but another image was misting over it, like a breath across the glass.

It wasn't his tallychamber.

Pieter stared through the window at a place far, far away. A place he had not seen for Bloom and Swoon and many a moon. A place he still saw now and then in his dreams.

But not like this. This was no dream. It was a nightmare.

"What happened?" he whispered.

He felt Teresa lay a hand on his arm.

He heard her say, "They made the smart choice."

6

The City through the Window

Through the window, Pieter saw his home. The city of Eureka. The tall walls, the exam halls, the tallymarkets where things were not bought and sold, but taught and solved. The chessboard patterned plaza that led up to the Quantifax, the home of Eureka's wisest mathemagician, whose great golden domed palace sat on the highest hill of the city, gleaming like an enormous bald head.

But it was just the city Pieter saw, and nothing else. The halls were empty, the tallymarkets deserted. Nobody walked the crumbling roads that lay cracked and dusty in the sun. If he squinted, Pieter noticed the gold paint had peeled off the roof of the Quantifax, showing the white bleached stone beneath. It looked like the half-buried skull of a giant. The lifeless streets below it were like a jumble of old bones.

The city was a graveyard.

"Eureka doesn't exist anymore," he heard Teresa say. "That's the truth. That's why you have to fight."

"The Czar broke his promise," said Amnabushka. "Czars always do."

"He told your parents they'd be safe if they surrendered you," Teresa said. "But he lied. After he took you, he poisoned Eureka's water wells with the Black Death."

Now Pieter noticed the boarded-up windows of each darkened house, and the red cross of plague painted upon every door. Cross after cross after red cross, like the city had taken a test and made mistake after mistake after mistake.

"The Black Death?" Pieter shook his head. It didn't make sense. The Czar kept just one vial of that deadly plague sealed away in his fortress to the north as a weapon of last resort. "He always says he'll only use it in defense, if Petrossia is attack—"

He stopped himself. Another of the Czar's lies. *One that everyone believed. But there had been more than one vial, he realized. More than one drop saved, ready to destroy an enemy.* He could see it with his own eyes: the Czar used it like a weapon—a weapon that killed whole cities that threatened him. And no one in Petrossia knew.

"You were the only survivor," Teresa said, touching his arm. "I'm so sorry."

Pieter couldn't speak. He couldn't think. He could only stare at the city through the window. It was like looking at a sum he didn't understand. His parents, his tutors, his class . . . they were all gone. There was just him now. One last mathemagician in all the world.

More than sadness, he felt anger. It rushed into his head like alchemy, dissolving that tiny stubborn part of him that had still wanted just to serve the Czar and survive.

"Being clever didn't save them," he said eventually, his mind changed. "*I* didn't save them." He looked up from the window's surface, a strange feeling in the center of his chest: utter, unshakable, hard-as-stone certainty. "But I can still save others," he said. "We can still beat the Czar."

Amnabushka touched her glass cat's eye again, and wiped Eureka from the glass. "Now he sees," she said to Teresa. "Now his mind is opened. Start your experimenting again, my Patra. This time you will succeed."

Teresa threw her arms around Amna. "Our very own fairy folkmother. You've saved us."

The old sweep cackled and coughed. "Quickly, then," she said, pushing them both toward the books and the equipment. "Three days left, and much to do."

Pieter nodded. He put away his thoughts of Eureka and his parents. Every bit of his brain was focused on the potion they needed to make.

Flutter and hum, wriggle of thumb—Amnabushka Baba Gale cast her peekaboo again and raised up her shawl. The door closed with a quiet click, and she was gone.

Pieter and Teresa were too busy experimenting to notice.

7

Grimaldi's Recipe, with Diagrams and Everything

Making the growth potion turned out to be totally impossible—but only a *little* bit impossible. To succeed, Pieter and Teresa would have to break several Laws of Reality.

This is not impossible to do. The laws that govern reality are like a flock of grazing sheep. Most of the time, they stand around, safe in the knowledge that gravity makes things fall, and $E=MC^2$, and the grass they are chewing is green.

But Pieter's genius and Teresa's imagination pounced on them like wolves, and suddenly all of reality was running around in panic, and in that chaos Up was Down, and E was the square root of minus one, and the grass they munched on wasn't green anymore and actually made of socks. Anything was possible.

So it was that two days from the end of Dismember, Pieter and Teresa made their breakthrough.

It happened at nine of the morn. Teresa was busy dissecting an apple seed (she was sure that inside there'd be a clue as to how tiny things grew bigger). Pieter, meanwhile, was methodically searching through Alchemaster Blüstav's books, page by page. Each one was stuffed full of alchemical recipes and inventions—most of them either unfathomable, or useless.

"This is all about turning iron to silver. Didn't work out so well for Blüstav."

"Can't read this one. Nice pictures though."

"Well, Teresa, if we ever want to know how to make a fartsichord, this is just the book we need."[15]

He heaved the book back on the shelf, hauled off the next one, and yelled out.

Teresa glanced up from her apple pip dissection, eyes blinking big as saucers behind a pair of scopical glasses. "Either you've seen a truly gigantic spider crawl out from the shelves, or you've discovered something interesting," she said.

"Interesting!" Pieter cried, lugging over the book. His hands shook. "Very, *very* interesting!"

---

15. A fartsichord is a type of piano with brass horns that instead of producing musical notes makes the most dreadful smells.

There it was on the page, written in long spidery scrawl. With diagrams and everything.

A Recipe for Size

1. *Take the shell of an acorn, this will be your cauldron*
2. *Into the acorn shell put:*
   - *a strand of hair (for hair grows long)*
   - *a shoot of bamboo (for bamboo grows tall)*
   - *and a smile (for smiles grow wide)*
3. *Mix together*

"Is that it?" Pieter was gobsmacked. It seemed so simple. "Only three instructions?"

Teresa shook her head in disbelief. She scrutinized the book's front cover. "All this time, and the answer was already scribbled down a hundred years before by some old bearded man with a cloak and an unpronounceable name."

"*Libra Gargantua*," read Pieter slowly. "By Grimaldi the Most Wise. I think you threw that at my head once."

"Well it wasn't very good at knocking you out, but it *might* be useful now," said Teresa, plonking the book down by the cauldron. "It's worth a go, isn't it? At least we won't wreck another cauldron. Look around for a shell of an acorn, Pieter."

He rushed to the window. It was the second-to-last day of Dismember, and below the North Spire the trees in the Winter Gardens all had leaves the color of flame.

"There!" he said, pointing beyond the ivy maze. "Look, Teresa!"

She jostled him to one side so she could see. "You sure that's an elder oak? Not a rattlesnoak?"

Pieter squinted, trying to see for sure. It was an elder oak—rattlesnoaks shook their acorns like maracas, to warn away any woodcutters who might be thinking of chopping them down.

"But how do we go and get one?" he wondered. "The Czar ordered us to stay here in the laboratory. If we're caught in the gardens it's a certain probability that we'll be—"

"Pieter," Teresa interrupted sternly. "For once in your life, stop being a genius and just use your imagination."

"All right," he said uncertainly. "Maybe we could ask Amnabushka to sing a spell to a bird, so it brings me one?"

But Amna wasn't bringing them dinner for another nine hours, and they both got bored of waiting.

In the end, they trained a mouse.[16]

16. This was easier than it sounds. Pieter just stuck a fluffy sock onto its tail, and Teresa convinced the mouse that it was a squirrel. Fetching acorns then became second nature to it.

After a few hours, the mouse (he was white with red eyes. Teresa wanted to call him Nuttikins) had collected a little pile of acorn-cauldrons on their table. It sat beside them, nibbling one, watching the alchemists work and listening to every word.

"What next?"

"A strand of hair—*ouch*!"

"There we are. Got a whole handful!"

"Now what?"

"A bamboo shoot . . ."

"Any in the Winter Gardens?"

"Not that I can see."

"Ah-ha, look at this!"

"Wow. That suit of pockets really has got everything."

Carefully, they halved an acorn's shell and poured the ingredients in. The strand of hair, they coiled up. The bamboo shoot, they ground to sawdust. It took them longer to figure out how to take a smile from their lips, but Teresa worked it out eventually. When Amna came up with dinner, they sent her to fetch the Czar's copy of the *Mona Lisa* (plundered from Prais) and carefully cut out her canvas mouth. They extracted the paint into a spirit solution and poured it carefully into their tiny cauldron.

"There might be a slim chance this could actually work,"

Pieter said, heart racing. He glued the acorn back together, and shook it to mix the ingredients. "It hasn't blown up yet, at least."

"That can only be a good sign." Teresa looked around. "What do we test it on?"

At one and the same time, their gaze fell on Nuttikins.

"Here, squirrel-squirrel-squirrel," said Teresa, holding out the acorn to the mouse with the fluffy sock tail. "Time for dessert."

Nuttikins sniffed at the acorn, then snatched it and nibbled it up.

Pieter and Teresa took a step back, held their breath . . .

And then.

Nothing.

Happened.

"Oh well." Pieter turned away. "Unlike the last ten cauldrons, Nuttikins didn't blow up. At least we've learned how to not make things explode."

The anticipation lighting up Teresa's face snuffed out like a swatted tinderfly. She stomped off to sulk.

"Grimaldi the Not So Wise, more like," she muttered at the book, slamming the cover shut and sending Nuttikins scurrying away in fright. "He's another fraud, just like Blüstav! Are there any alchemists who aren't liars? How do they get away with it? I suppose you can get away with almost anything once you've been dead for long enough."

And that was it.

Yesterday, before he'd seen Eureka, Pieter's brain would have let Teresa's remark go. But not now. Now he shouted out suddenly.

Teresa looked up. "Either you've stubbed your toe," she said, "or you've realized something extremely important."

"Extremely important!" he cried. "Teresa, you're right!"

"I am?"

Pieter went straight back to the book and opened it up. "Grimaldi wrote this recipe years and years ago—but what's it done since his death?"[17]

"Got dusty?" Teresa suggested.

"Got *bigger*!" he said. "That's what a growth potion does, isn't it? And doesn't it make sense that the *recipe* would grow bigger too? It's simple mathemagics: the list of ingredients is increasing. It might have worked back in the time of Grimaldi, but now . . ."

Teresa let out an excited shriek. "Pieter, you're right! I'm

---

17. Actually, Grimaldi wasn't dead. Six hundred years ago, he had discovered the elixir of eternal life. Unfortunately, after he drank the potion that would make him live for ever, the alchemist realized that although he couldn't die, he could still grow older. Frantically, Grimaldi tried to discover the elixir of eternal youth, but by the time he invented that, he was already three hundred years old, and his body was so ancient it was nothing but a skeleton.

running the list of instructions through my head right now, and I can't help adding more and more ingredients. Quick, write this all down!"

Pieter grabbed a quill, and underneath Grimaldi's recipe he scrawled the following:

A Recipe for Size

1. *Take the shell of an acorn, this will be your cauldron*
2. *Into the acorn shell put:*
   - *a strand of hair (for hair grows long)*
   - *a shoot of bamboo (for bamboo grows tall)*
   - *and a smile (for smiles grow wide)*
3. *Mix together*

THEN . . .

4. *Extract the grow from a growl, the must from a mustache, the you from a layout, and the big from a bridge.*
5. *Add to the acorn in the correct order: You, Must, Grow, Big.*
6. *When drinking, take six sips, wait for six seconds, then stand on your head (for 6 gets bigger when you turn it upside down).*

"Hurry!" Teresa said breathlessly. "We have to make it before the list gets even longer!"

They worked through the night. Crack the acorn shell and peel. Curl, poke, and prod. Chop that bamboo stalk to dust. Just a sprinkle. Growl, don't wheeze! Just one moment, Amna, please! Would you mind . . . ? Could you find . . . ? Stir it slowly—do it clockwise—hours turn from small to big. Keep it steady. Almost ready. Nuttikins? Come take a swig!

But Nuttikins was sleeping somewhere, in his nest behind the wall. Nowhere to be seen at all.

So sometime after dawn, Teresa fetched a pair of tiny tweezers and searched for something really small.

A bit of dirt? A speck of dust? An itty-bitty fleck of rust? Or what about this grain of sand? Perfect! Keep it in your hand.

Grip steady now . . .

Don't let it slip . . .

Tip out the potion . . .

Just a drip . . .

Dab it in, nice and slow . . .

Turn it over . . .

Watch it *GROW*!

First double-sized, and now it's treble! Now the grain's become a pebble! It works, it works just as we planned! It really made the sand expand!

Gargantua works—just in time! Come morn, it is the Czar's deadline. . . .

That last night of Dismember they lay in their beds, made from stacked books and blankets, and whispered in the light of the tinderfly, too excited to sleep.

"No turning back now," Teresa whispered. "By the end of winter, the palace will either have a new ruler, or three more heads spiked on the gatehouse walls."

Pieter smiled. He knew which outcome was the most probable. They had done it. Their alchemy was finished, and it worked.

"In one way, I can't wait for tomorrow," Teresa said, her eyes shining green in the light. "But I also wish we could do this, and stay in this laboratory, forever."

"We can," said Pieter. "After the Czar is gone, you'll be Royal Alchemaster to Alexander, won't you? And we'll work on a way to turn him back to a boy that doesn't involve waiting decades for the Catastrophica to wear off, and then we'll make other potions. Potions to turn sick people well, and sad people happy. And then, when we grow up, we'll go to

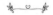

Eureka and rebuild the city. I'll teach mathemagics, you'll teach alchemy."

Teresa smiled sleepily. "What about Amnabushka?"

"She can teach magic. As long as she stops calling you her Patra all the time. Why does she do that, anyway?"

Teresa gave him a snooty look and balanced a cup upside down on her head as if it were the Iron Crown. "Because I'm a princess," she said in a posh voice, and yawned. "Now close your eyes and go to sleep! Hurry, serf! Your Royal Highness demands it!"

Pieter grinned as he settled down in his bed. "You swore you'd stop fibbing to me," he muttered, just before she started to snore.

It wasn't until the month of Yule, when Pieter lay in the most dreadful of the Czar's dungeons, that he realized that Teresa had kept her promise.

8

Wompf!

At seven of the morn on the last day of Dismember, Pieter kicked off his blankets and helped Teresa shrug on her Alchemaster robes, heavy as curtains. Ugor came to take them from the laboratory. With the acorn tight in his fist, Pieter came down from the North Spire with Teresa by his side.

"Ow," she whispered next to him. "Ow. Ow."

He looked sideways at her. "Why are you pinching yourself?"

"Because I can hardly believe I'm awake."

There beside her, Pieter felt the same. He supposed he should have been terrified, but instead he drifted down the stairs as if in a dream. Through the windows, the dim swirly sky outside was on the cusp of both autumn and winter, night and day, stormy and calm.

This was the moment when everything would change

forever. Pieter knew it was. And he was sure it was a change for the better too.

The plan was set. The potion was ready.

What could possibly go wrong?

Ugor marched them down the corridors ("Good luck!" Amna mouthed as they passed her dusting the windows), and together they entered the Royal Chamber.

"Time's up, Tallymaster." The Czar sat at his breakfast table, scalping the tops off his ostrich eggs with Viktor. "Are you sure this will work?"

Pieter had not seen the Czar since before Amna's spell had shown him the ruins of Eureka. He bowed low, to hide his anger.

"One hundred percent," he said, fighting hard to keep the hatred from his voice. "I'm certain the potion will succeed." *Just not in the way you think it will, you murderous thug*, he added in his head.

"I hope," said the Czar, with a mouthful of ostrich egg, "that you don't disappoint yourself. Because that would mean disappointing *me*."

The butler brought Prince Alexander in from his newly furnished bedroom, where all the wallpaper was scratch proof, and the floor was covered with the white gravel of cat litter. He jumped off his velvet cushion as soon as he saw Pieter and Teresa, and bounded over.

"Alexander! We missed you!" They both rushed forward to give him a cuddle.

"No stroking His Royal Fluffiness," growled Ugor, stepping in front of them.

Teresa scowled and backed away, but Pieter wasn't feeling so timid anymore.

Tired? Perhaps.

Terrified? A little.

But one way or the other, he was through with being told what to do. So he simply ducked under Ugor's legs, scooped up the purring prince, and said to the butler: "Bring His Young Majesty a saucer of milk!"

The command raced through the servants, fast as lightning, until finally in came the butler and there it was on the blood-red carpet: a cool, white saucer of milk.

The Czar narrowed his eyes. *He* was accustomed to giving the orders around here. But he let his irritation go. He was desperate to solve the problem of his son, and these alchemists might just have the solution.

"Do it," he ordered.

Pieter handed the acorn to Teresa. "It should be you," he said. "It's your alchemy."

Fingers trembling, she took the Gargantua and went over to the milk. She cracked the shell between two breakfast spoons, shaking a single drop of the Gargantua potion into the saucer. Then she stepped back and nodded to Pieter, who put Prince Alexander down by the dish.

He sniffed it with his little pink nose, and then, with his little pink tongue, he began to lap up the milk.

For a long time, that was the only sound: the *splish-splash-splosh* of Prince Alexander drinking his saucer of milk. Teresa and Pieter looked on, hoping and praying. The Czar narrowed his eyes. Ugor held his breath.

And then.

Nothing.

Happened.

"OFF WITH THEIR HEADS!" roared the Czar, hurling his breakfast fork at Pieter. It whizzed just past his nose and jammed in the door, quivering.

"Wait!" cried Teresa, and before Ugor could grab her, she darted forward and seized the prince by the scruff of the neck.

"GET HER!" roared Ugor, and from various hiding places leaped the Czar's famous and rarely seen bodyguards.

The Slinjas.

The Slinjas were the Czar's deadliest and most secret of soldiers. Through years of agonizing training under the heaviest of weights, they squashed themselves down until they were flattened completely. The most dedicated were as thin as sheets of paper. Being so thin, they carried no weapons, but instead dipped their hands in cobra venom. A wound from a Slinja could be as slight as a papercut but far deadlier.[18]

At Ugor's command, the Slinjas emerged, brandishing their poisoned fingertips. There was one hiding behind the curtains, one beneath the floorboards, and one who had hidden amongst the breakfast things by squeezing into the pepperpot.

"Put down the fluffy-wuffy-kitty-witty!" they called out. Their voices were like the whisper of willow rushes by the banks of the Ossia.

"I won't hurt him," said Teresa. "I just forgot something."

And then, just as the recipe advised, she finished counting to six, and stood the prince on his head.

WOMPF!

That was the sound in the room when it happened: everyone said so afterward. The prince grew *bigger* in every which way: he went tall and wide and long. He sort of exploded, whilst staying in one piece. And then he stopped exploding out, and just stayed the same size. Which, at the end of it all, was roughly the size of a lion.

---

18. Slinjas also underwent considerable training to resist the urge to pick their noses.

Everyone in the room stepped back a little, especially Bloodbath, who was now just a paw swipe away from a kitten ten times his size.

"UNBELIEVABLE!" cried the Czar. "IT WORKS! LET ME TRY!"

Seizing the open acorn from Teresa's grasp, he sprinkled Gargantua all over the table and gave it a sharp kick, turning bits of his breakfast upside down.

WOMPF! WOMPF! WOMPF!

The ostrich eggs became enormous speckled boulders.

A silver fork sprang up to the size of a trident.

A banana wobbled back and forth, big as a curved yellow canoe.

Finally, the table legs couldn't take any more weight and collapsed with a crash.

With a laugh so loud it made the buckling table legs sound like twigs breaking, the Czar bounded toward his son.

"MY BOY!" he roared with approval. "JUST LOOK AT HOW YOU'VE GROWN!"

Alexander raised a paw at his father. Out slid claws, each as long and deadly as a dagger.

"Finally," said the Czar proudly, tousling his fingers through Alexander's fur. "You're a conqueror fit to be my heir. I'm proud of you."

It was perhaps the nicest thing the Czar had ever said to his son. Alexander's tail swished, his ears twitched, and from his throat there came a deep purr, like marbles rattling in a jar.

"Well done, my Alchemaster and Tallymaster," the Czar boomed. He stood in his gleaming armor, with his lion-kitten son beside him. His eyes were full of plans—plans of conquest and dominion.

"Take them back to the laboratory!" he said to Ugor. "Get them everything they need." He grinned at Pieter and Teresa. "You will repeat your alchemy. You will make him even *bigger*. I want Alexander to conquer giants, titans . . . even gods! I will not stop until my son plays with elephants as if they were mice!"

Across the empire, the news spread. All Hail Alexander, the All-Conquering Kitten! There were celebrations throughout Petrossia, from Muscov to Xanderberg. Ginger confetti rained in the streets, men groomed their mustaches into whiskers, and ladies sewed little triangles of felt onto their bonnets, as if they had cat ears.

In the Winter Palace laboratory, Pieter and Teresa celebrated too. Amna brought them up three mugs from the kitchens, and sang a spell to make the sugar cubes dance across the table and plop themselves in the tea. The three of them toasted the imminent success of Operation: *His Royal Whiskers.*

"Many and many a time I had my doubts about you, Pieter Abadabacus," Amna said. "But where would my manners be now if I didn't sing your praises?"

Pieter blushed. "Thank you," he said. "We did it together. You plus me plus Teresa."

She nudged him. "Don't forget Nuttikins."

They clonked their mugs together. "To Nuttikins!"

"When do we tell Alexander the plan?" Pieter asked. He was already thinking ahead to when the Czar would be overthrown and cast down into his own dungeons. He was going to enjoy sentencing the bloodthirsty tyrant to the most terrible torture imaginable.[19]

"I can sweep my way into his room tonight," said Amna, "and tell him to pounce."

"Do it," Teresa said. "But tell him to hold off until we give the signal. He needs to be *bigger*, just like the Czar told us."

Amna touched the reindeer's tooth in her hair. "Careful, my Patra. The bigger the prince, the bigger the consequences."

"I know that. But I won't allow Alexander to fight unless there's absolutely no way he could possibly be hurt. We only

19. It involved lots of apologizing, and giving up all his armies and crowns, and having Viktor melted down into something harmless like a kettle.

get one chance at this—we have to be certain he can win."

Pieter shrugged. Teresa was right: another few doses of Gargantua couldn't do any harm. They might as well enlarge Alexander until he could knock away Viktor with one flick and trap the Czar under his paw.

"Pass another acorn, then," he said. "Let's get brewing."

PART THREE

Empurrer

Those who'll play with cats must
expect to be scratched.

—*DON QUIXOTE*, MIGUEL DE CERVANTES

Psychopomp | 'sʌɪkə(ʊ)pɒmp | *Noun*
A guide for souls to the land of the dead.

(A NOTE ON STUPIDITY)

Most people think that geniuses are not capable of stupidity. In fact, the opposite is true. The brain of a genius is simply capable of more than other brains, which not only means they can be smarter than everyone else, but also *stupider.*

This is what makes a genius one of the most dangerous creatures on Earth. It is their habit of having the most incredible ideas without thinking through the consequences that makes them so lethal. On the list of the World's Deadliest Animals, a genius could easily make it into the Top 10, depending on how much thinking they were doing that day.

At that moment, Pieter and Teresa were currently joint-third on the list—just below the remaining vial of the Black Death plague that had wiped out Eureka. The Czar, of course, still held the number one spot. For now.

But there was another creature steadily climbing the ranks, who was growing more dangerous—and more enormous—by the day.

1

Five Doses of Gargantua

The first week of Welkin was full of changes. The days turned shorter and drearier; the nights grew glittering and cold. Down from the wild northern Waste, the wind began its slow unceasing wail, that would stretch on through Welkin and rise to a shriek when Worsen came, until it got so loud and piercing it would sometimes shatter windows, like an opera singer's high note.

But it was Alexander that changed most of all.

On Mournday, he was lion-sized.

By Toilsday, he was oliphant-sized.

By Warsday, he was whale-sized.

By Czarsday, he was dinosaur-sized.

By Firday, after his fifth dose of the Gargantua potion, Prince Alexander was beyond colossal.

He entered and exited the Winter Palace in a specially made cat flap that was seventy feet high. He napped in the Hall of Faces—the only room he could now fit into—leaning his head on a tremendous pillow that had been stuffed with the wool of a hundred flocks of sheep. Since Warsday, the Czar had taken to sleeping on the prince: he would lie down in the fur that was long and reddish-golden, and rippled like corn in the breeze.

Alexander could leap across the River Ossia in a single bound. He could outrun the wind, and unhorse a hundred knights with one swipe. His meow could be heard in far and distant countries, where it was mistaken for the sound of the end of the world. And perhaps it was, for as he grew ever bigger, Alexander's thirst grew ever more insatiable.

He had stopped drinking his milk out of saucers, buckets, and bathtubs—they were far too small. Instead, he drank from the Fountain of Sobs in the palace courtyard, which had been disconnected from its usual water supply and hooked up to the udders of a herd of cows.

The prince's appetite, too, had grown just as enormous as he had. By Czarsday, Alexander was devouring a herd of cows for breakfast, a shoal of fish for lunch, and an entire murder of crows for supper.

After four days of his guzzling, the River Ossia was almost empty, the hills were bare, and the forests were silent. Alexander was hoovering up every last scrap of food in the

kingdom. Having eaten every animal for miles around, he was now starting on the poor creatures in the small zoo that formed part of the palace gardens. On Firday, Alexander gobbled up a camel, some flamingos, two koala bears, a firebird (which gave him heartburn), a bilebear (which gave him a stomachache) and a puffin (which made him out of breath).

After dinner, several rare species the Czar had plundered from exotic lands—including two pygmy tigers, a gold-feathered chicken that laid Fabergé eggs, and a glacier slug that Alexander nibbled on like a popsicle stick—were suddenly extinct.

The people in Petrossia were growing nervous.

So were Pieter and Teresa.

"I think it's time we told Alexander to pounce," Teresa said when they woke on the second week of Welkin. "He's *got* to be big enough now, and besides, I'm getting impatient."

"I'm getting hungry," said Pieter, deciding now was the time to bring up a problem nagging him. There was simply not enough food now that Petrossia had Alexander's enormous belly to fill. Pieter had tried to solve the problem as best as he could, using mathemagics. Hunched over a list of all the stores left in the Winter Palace kitchens, he split turnips into tiny fractions, or divided not enough eggs between too many people. He multiplied milk by mixing in water, he added sawdust to flour.

No one had starved, but everyone was miserable. They'd had nothing but beetroot soup and butterless bread since Czarsday. By the Czar's decree, what meat was left was now only to be eaten by Himself and Alexander.

Pieter looked down into the courtyard. Up from the basement kitchens, cooks were wheeling huge barrows piled high with food. Sausages, roast beef, bacon, and blood pudding . . . all heading toward the Hall of Faces.

Teresa feasted her eyes on the parade of deliciousness passing beneath them. Then she slapped her hand to her head and laughed. "Pieter, we're fools!" she said. "The solution's easy: the Czar even showed it to us on Mournday! Why don't we just use the Gargantua on Alexander's *food*?"

In a few moments, she had latched on a grapple to the sill and rappelled out the window. Pieter passed her a fork tied to a yardstick, and like a spider on a thread, Teresa dropped down the North Spire and speared a garlic sausage from a passing barrow. Up she winched herself, while Pieter got Nuttikins to fetch one of the dozen acorns of Gargantua potion they had spent all week brewing. Teresa shook the sausage off the fork and onto a plate, cracked the acorn that

Pieter passed her, and the two of them stepped back and waited for the *WOMPF*.

It took a long time to come.

Too long.

Something was wrong. Why wasn't the sausage bigger? It ought to have swelled to the size of a well-fed boa constrictor.

"Did you remember to turn it upside down?" Pieter asked.

"Of course I did," Teresa said. "Must have been a bad nut. Or a silly sausage. Get Nuttikins to fetch another acorn, and we'll try again."

But the next acorn didn't work either. None of them worked. Not on the sausage, not on the lamb chop, not on anything else Teresa rappelled down to fetch.

The potion's list of ingredients had grown again. Teresa's Gargantua recipe was now just as useless and incomplete as Grimaldi's original recipe had been.

"We can solve it!" Teresa insisted. "Just like we did last time. We just need to add a few dozen more things. . . ."

Pieter groaned. "By the time we've done that, there won't *be* any more food to enlarge. Alexander will have gobbled it all up, and everyone in Petrossia will starve."

The two friends looked at each other in stunned silence. They had set out to save Petrossia from the Czar's conquering—had they ended up dooming it to Alexander's appetite?

"That's it, then," said Teresa, rushing over to shrug on her Alchemaster robes. "We have to get Alexander to overthrow the Czar *right now.* And then we have to start shrinking him back down to size, before it's too late."

2

Meowtiny

The Winter Palace fireplaces were always kept roaring and stoked in the cold Welkin weather, so Teresa could not climb down the chimneys to visit Alexander in secret. The only time they saw the prince was each breakfast, when they came with the acorn to crack into his morn milk.

Luckily, Amna had already managed to explain Operation: *His Royal Whiskers* to Alexander on Toilsday when she had swept his room. Everything was set. All Pieter and Teresa had to do was yell out "MEOWTINY!" as loud as they could, and the prince would pounce on the Czar.

It sounded easy as counting one-two-three.

So why did Pieter suddenly feel so nervous?

Pieter and Teresa followed their guards down the corridor to the Hall of Faces. The Czar was in there, clipping his son's claws with garden shears. Pieter's breath caught at the size of Alexander. He was stretched out on the floor, snoozing happily. A rumbling, rising-and-falling orange-furred mountain. His purr sounded like distant drilling, as if deep within his belly there were dwarves mining for gold. He did not even wake when Pieter and Teresa entered. They must have been about as distracting as scurrying ants.

"Alchemaster! Tallymaster!" said the Czar. His smile gleamed bright as his armor. "I am so pleased with your work! I knew I was right to spare your lives!" He put down the shears and gestured to his vast son.

Pieter and Teresa glanced nervously at each other. Should they shout now? Should they wait until Alexander was awake? What if they didn't yell "MEOWTINY!" loud enough, and the prince carried on snoozing?

"You are indeed masters of alchelements," grinned the Czar. "I am envious. I have only mastered one element—the element of surprise. Let me demonstrate. Come in, Spymaster!"

He turned to face the stained-glass doors. They creaked open, and something entered the hall.

It was a ball.

A small ball.

A small ball, all made of wire.

It rolled across the flagstone floor toward them, like a soccer ball dribbled by a ghost, until the Czar stopped it with his boot.

A hatch on the wire ball's surface swung outward, and a small white something scurried out. He wore worn leather boots, a floppy hat with a blue budgie feather tucked into the brim, and a small toothpick of a sword strapped to his side. He perched on the wire ball for a moment, panting as he caught his breath, and blinking his red eyes.

"Highness," said the small white something.

Pieter blinked. Teresa gawped.

"Nuttikins!" cried Teresa.

"Nuttikins?" cried Pieter.

"Also known as Sir Klaus the Mousketeer," the Czar corrected. "My Spymaster."

Pieter gawped at the mysterious member of the War Council he had never seen before. Except he *had* seen him—many times. The Spymaster had hidden in plain sight.

Sitting on his wire ball, Sir Klaus twitched his whiskers. "Alchemists," the mouse said, shaking his head. "So wrapped up in their own thinking, they miss what is right beneath their noses."

Pieter and Teresa both looked at each other and yelled out together: "He can *talk*?!"

"Oh yes," said the Czar. "And he has told me everything. I know about Operation: *His Royal Whiskers*, I know about the old Baba Sister who's been helping you with her witchery, and I know the Gargantua potion is useless."

Pieter's heart went slack.

"Also," the Czar added, "I hear you stole a sausage."

"Firstly," began Teresa, "that was for scientific purposes. Secondly, I didn't do it. Thirdly, MEOWTINY!"

Her voice echoed round the rafters. Alexander's purring snores rumbled on. Pieter shot Teresa a nervous glance.

"MEOWTINY!" they both bellowed together.

The prince's ears twitched in his sleep. That was all. Why didn't he wake?

"Snoozeweed in his milk, and cotton wool in his ears," the Czar explained with a smile. "Not that I didn't trust my own son not to betray me, but still . . . it's wise to take precautions."

Then he clicked his fingers, and the Slinjas slid out from behind the Hall of Faces portraits. In an eyeblink, Pieter and Teresa were surrounded.

"I have to admit," the Czar said, "I'm impressed. The two of you might not be strong, but you *are* imaginative. I respect that. Imagination is its own sort of power. And with it, you came close—closer than anyone has ever come before—to defeating me."

"You're wrong," Teresa said, as she and Pieter stood back-to-back while the Slinjas closed in. "Imagination isn't our power. It's friendship."

Pieter said nothing. *Keep him talking, Teresa. The longer he talks, the more chance there is that Alexander might wake.*

"Friendship? You think friendship is a power?" The Czar's laugh was like an artillery barrage. It made Pieter wince.

And it made Alexander's enormous tree-trunk tail twitch.

He nudged Teresa. No need—she'd seen it too.

"Let me show you what true power is," said the Czar, and he clicked his fingers again.

The Slinjas moved fast.

Teresa moved faster.

Pieter moved fastest of all.

As the Slinjas came toward them, feet whispering over the floor, Teresa threw a fistful of hazelnuts to trip them. But Pieter shoved her, and they flew over the heads of the bodyguards, and landed straight in the fire that roared in the hearth.

"Pieter! You made me *miss*!"

"No, I didn't," he said, as in the fireplace, the cooking hazelnuts started to pop.

Bang! Crackle! Snap! It was like a small fireworks display had commenced inside the hearth. Toasted hazelnuts flew into the hall, smelling of burnt sugar and smoke. Drawn up from the depths of his dreams by the noise and the aroma, Alexander opened one enormous green eye. There was a swishing sound, like a field of wheat in Swoon, as he sat up and pawed at his head. Huge white tufts of cotton wool fell from his ears, wafting in the air like clouds.

Then the prince looked down, and saw his best friends in danger.

"MEOWTINY!" Pieter and Teresa shouted the word as loudly and desperately as they could.

The Czar let out a bellow of anger. His midnight cape billowed as he whirled round, drawing Viktor.

Alexander sent the sword spinning from his father's grasp with the flick of one claw. It hit the floor, *clatter* and *clang*. Before he could pick up his blade, the Czar found himself gently pinned to the floor by his son's enormous paw.

Even the Slinjas stopped to stare.

For the first time ever, the Czar had just been beaten. Without moving his paw, Alexander swung his mighty tail across the flagstones. Pieter and Teresa leaped back as the tidal wave of ginger fur swept half the Slinjas to one side. The rest of them turned sideways and posted themselves through the door crack, vanishing away.

The tumult died down, until the only sounds were the

papery scrabblings of the Slinjas slapped flat against the far wall, the mighty sigh of Alexander's vast lungs, and Pieter's own stunned heartbeat hammering hard in his chest.

Operation: *His Royal Whiskers* was complete.

Pop! went the last of the hazelnuts.

"See?" Teresa said to the Czar at last. "It doesn't matter how weak you are. If you have friends, they'll lend you their strength."

Pieter thought the Czar would either be too furious or too stunned to reply. But despite the fact that he was disarmed and held firmly to the floor, he did not look trapped or beaten.

Instead, he was smiling.

"Perhaps," he said, voice strained beneath the weight of Alexander. "But you've forgotten one thing."

Teresa scowled. "What's that?"

And then she froze, and Pieter felt something clamber onto his shoulder.

"Me," said Sir Klaus.

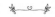

Going unnoticed is the talent of all mice, and Sir Klaus had honed that particular skill to deadly perfection. The minute the fight had started, he had slipped from sight and mind completely, just as he always did. Now the Spymaster had suddenly reappeared, drawing his sword like a silver blade of grass. He held the point to Pieter's neck.

"Release the Czar, Young Majesty," Sir Klaus said to the prince. "Now."

Alexander hissed at the mouse. The noise was so deafening, it made Pieter rock back on his heels slightly. Teresa edged forward a fraction. Just another few steps and she could reach out and—

"Stay where you are, traitor." Sir Klaus held up a paw to her. "Lord Xin has coated my sword with the cobra venom of the Slinjas. Take another step, and the Tallymaster will be dead in a dozen heartbeats."

Teresa clenched her fists in helpless rage. "How can you do this?" she said to the mouse. "I fed you crumbs and nibbles every day."

Sir Klaus's voice was pained, but his grip on his sword did not waver. "You showed me much kindness, it is true. But I am a knight, in sworn service to the Czar. If I break my oath, I am no knight at all. Now tell the prince to free His Majesty."

"Don't worry, son," sneered the Czar from beneath Alexander's paw. "When you release me, nothing bad will happen to Pieter and Teresa. Or to that Baba Sister. I'm going to take good care of all three of them. They're my guarantee that from now on, you'll do *exactly* as I say. You wouldn't want anything to happen to them, would you?"

Teresa slumped her shoulders. "Do it, Alexander. Let the Czar go."

Alexander began to lift away his paw, freeing his father. The Czar looked triumphant as he began to wriggle free . . .

"ALEXANDER, WAIT!"

Pieter's shout echoed through the hall. Confused, the enormous paw pressed down again. *Oof!* went the Czar, as he slammed back to the floor.

Teresa stared at him. "Pieter, what are you doing?"

The answer was simple mathemagics. "Alexander has the Czar. Sir Klaus has me. That evens out. *But no one has you yet, Teresa.* You have to run!"

She gave him one of her looks (the one with the narrowed eyes and the scorn). "I'm going nowhere. We're in this together, for better or worse. That's what being friends means."

Behind them, the doors to the hall opened. Lord Xin appeared, with his curved claw of a dagger, and Ugor with his blundergun. They began to edge forward, step by step. Pieter had only a few seconds left to convince her.

"I won't leave Alexander!" Teresa insisted. "Or Amna! Or *you*!"

"There is no me!" Pieter cried. "There's no Alexander, no Amna, only *us*! And if you escape, then *we're* still twenty-five percent free! We've got twenty-five percent more of a chance! Twenty-five percent more hope!" Normally, Teresa Gust didn't care for percentage-based arguments. But this time, Pieter's reasoning made perfect sense.

"I'll come back," she whispered. "I'll save you all. I promise."

Pieter nodded, a lump in his throat. Alexander dipped his head. His great green-flecked eyes were speckled with tears and pain, like cathedral windows in the rain.

"Halt!" cried Sir Klaus, sword at Pieter's neck. "Halt, or he dies!"

"Let her go, fool!" roared the Czar from under Alexander's paw. "The Tallymaster's our only hostage—kill him and I'm doomed! Ugor and Lord Xin will deal with the girl!"

As the Warmaster and Heirmaster sprinted down the hall, Teresa ran to the roaring fireplace. She threw her Alchemaster robes on the flames to smother them just long enough for her to scrabble up the chimney. As Ugor reached the hearth, Teresa dumped a pocketful of cobflour back down the flue.

The white puff ignited—an enormous fireball burped from the hearth—and there was the sharp reek of burning hair. Ugor roared and toppled backwards, swatting at his knotted beard that had caught fire. Lord Xin sheared it off at the chin with his dagger, and stamped the flaming beard out on the floor.

When at last all the smoke cleared, Teresa Gust was gone.

Pieter never saw her again.

Not while they were both still alive, anyway.

3

In the Gloom Room

At first, the Gloom Room did not seem as bad as the other cells in the Czar's dungeon. It was not freezing cold, nor pitch-dark, nor was it full of things that shuffled over the floor and nibbled at your toes. It had no bars and no chains. Parts of it were almost comfortable. There was a fireplace, a rug. Even armchairs.

And yet the Gloom Room was, without a doubt, the most horrible and inescapable prison in all of Petrossia.

What was horrible about the Gloom Room was the *smell*.

It was a heavy, stifling stench that covered your face like a damp towel. A smell that sank your spirits and lowered your head and sent the tears spilling from your eyes.

It was the smell, believe it or not, of defeat.[20]

Defeat was in the gray carpet and the faded armchairs.

---

20. If you are wondering what defeat smells like, you could spend a day trying to race a cheetah, wrestle a bear, and outstare a goldfish. By midday, you'll know what defeat smells like: you.

It was in the beige wallpaper and the rust of the window bars and the way the fireplace did nothing but smolder and wheeze. It had wriggled into everywhere and everything, and if you were down in the Gloom Room, it was only a matter of time before it wriggled into you too.

Breathing it in, defeat would settle deep down in your chest, gnawing and nibbling away at the fighting part of you, until eventually you lay down and surrendered. You gave up your escape plans, handed over all hope, and you never thought of your freedom again.

No one had ever escaped from the Gloom Room.

Pieter and Amna had been prisoners in there, all through Welkin and Worsen.

"Wake up," Amnabushka said, elbowing him in the ribs.

Pieter groaned. He let the old sweep jab him. It was too much of a struggle to do anything now but lie in his armchair. "I *am* up," he said.

"Open those eyes then."

"I *can't*." Each word was a battle that was a little harder to fight. "My eyelids have given up. They keep sliding shut. I can't stop them."

"Tie your eyelashes to your eyebrows."

He tried. "My fingers have surrendered."

"So learn how to tie with your toes!" Amna whacked him hard. "I'm thousands of miles old, and you don't see me surrendering!"

Somehow, Pieter managed to force his eyes open and sit up. It took all his strength to stop himself from slumping back into his seat.

"This will cheer you up," Amna said, pointing outside. "Look."

Pieter peered past the frosted windowpane. Out in the freezing cold courtyard, guards were rolling a red carpet from the gate to the Hall of Faces, and an orkestar was playing carols. The musicians were practicing "The Forest Raised a Yuletide Tree," really fast so their fingers didn't freeze up and drop off. Crowds of Petrossia folk, wrapped up in reindeer hides, had gathered to watch. Banners were unfurling from the gatehouse towers and flapping in the wind like flayed skins. The spiked heads above the gate were decorated with iron tinsel.

Preparations for Yuletide: the day that marked the end of winter and the start of spring. Had they really been in the Gloom Room so long? Pieter had lost track of the date weeks ago. For the first time ever, he didn't count the days. There was no point. Each one was the same but a little worse.

Every time he opened his eyes now, the Gloom Room

looked a little more depressing. The wallpaper seemed more faded and curling; the armchairs, tattier; Amna's smile, a little thinner. She kept touching the emptiness at the end of her plaits. Lord Xin had cut all the charms from her hair. With them had gone her magic.

At Pieter's feet, Bloodbath whimpered and whined. The poor poodle's ransom was still too high for the Duke of Madri to pay, and so the Czar had tossed him into the Gloom Room along with them.

Most miserable-looking of all was Alexander. Though he was far too big to fit in the Gloom Room, Pieter still saw him every day. Each morn at six, the whole palace would tremor from enormous stomping footsteps, and the prince would appear in the courtyard and gaze in through the window at them. Pieter would pull back the curtains and stare back at the enormous green eyes outside to prove that he was still the Czar's hostage. Alexander would dip his head each time, and mewl louder and sadder than the wind moaning down the chimney.

"There's still hope," Amna whispered in his ear. "There's still my Patra."

That was true. Teresa had somehow not been caught and imprisoned along with them. Where could she be? Where had she gone? Pieter didn't know the answer. Not because there wasn't one, but because there were too many. For rumors are like sunrises, or tides upon the shore: no sooner do you count them all, there comes along one more.

This is what the guards whispered to themselves outside:

She was somewhere in Petrossia, she was a hundred miles away. Lord Xin was after her—no, she was after him. She had escaped a prison in Port Xanderberg, she was alive and well in Albion. She wore a white priest's gown, she had dyed her hair brown. She was coming to free the serfs, she was sailing west forever. She could turn into a cat. Grow enormous. Change the weather.

An alchemist? That wasn't true. She was a hero. Villain too. She was Petrossia's doom. Its savior. She had a friend, but he betrayed her. She's harder to catch than Sir Klaus! She's tougher than Ugor by far! Could it even be that she is mightier than the Czar?

On the rumors went. On and on.

Pieter had never quite believed in infinity. A number that can't be counted? It didn't add up. Still, there were several things that even mathemagicians quietly refused to keep an exact tally of and used vague terms for, like "masses," "oodles," and "umpteen."

The stars in the sky, or water in the ocean, or leaves in the forests.

To this list, Pieter found himself adding: *rumors about Teresa Gust.* And no matter how many he heard the guards whisper to one another outside the Gloom Room door, Pieter could never have enough. He strained his ears now, as the soldiers stationed by the door muttered.

"I heard she's in Albion, turning seagulls into soldiers with that alchemy of hers."

"That's all tittle-tat. The Warmaster chased her out onto the Waste, where the winds froze her solid."

Pieter shivered, and beside him Amna put a hand on his knee. "Don't worry," she whispered. "That's not true. I know that girl. Endless pockets, and ever another idea."

"She's the best player of hide-and-seek I know," said Pieter. As always, thinking of Teresa helped ward off the despair. "That has to help, doesn't it?"

"That it must. She knows how to stay hidden. Been doing it since the day she was born."

A thought occurred to Pieter. He still had not given up thinking, it seemed.

"You know where Teresa's from," he said.

Amna hesitated. "Don't."

"You do. 'Been doing it since the day she was born,' you said."

"Didn't."

"Liar. Tell me the truth."

"She's a lunar baby."

"I've heard that one."

"She's a bald monkey, and there was a coconut that she hatched from."

Pieter shook his head. "You're not even telling that one right. She's a bald monkey born at the top of a palm tree, and a big gale blew her down the chimney. . . ."

He trailed off.

A big gale . . .

"When we first met, you said you'd had three names, and three lives," Pieter said. "Before Amnabushka, you were Baba Gale, and before Baba Gale, you were a girl from Albion called . . ."

Amnabushka opened her mouth, then drew her lips tight like a drawstring purse.

"Abigail!" Pieter sat up, gasping. "A-big-gail blew her down the chimney! The story was a clue! *You're* her mother!"

Amna whacked him again, but only lightly. "Charmer. Count my wrinkles, Tallymaster. I'm old enough to be her great-grandbaba."

Pieter scrutinized her closely. "*Are* you?"

"No!"

He sank back into his armchair. For a moment he felt

like he'd almost solved the mystery of Teresa's origins. He supposed it would be pretty strange if Amna called her granddaughter her "Patra." He'd looked up the word, way back in Welkin—it came from Eglyph, and it meant "She Who Is Chosen."

"I'm going back to sleep, then," he sighed. "There's nothing worth staying up for—"

"No!" Amna's cry didn't even startle Bloodbath, who had evidently given up on being awake too. "If you go to sleep, you won't wake up, will you? You'll surrender completely, and the Pale Traveler will come to take your soul! I know it!"

Pieter said nothing. He listened to her think.

"If I tell you the truth, will you stay awake to listen?"

Pieter fluttered his eyes open a little, so she would know he would.

"Promise?" She shook him by the shoulders. "Swear?"

He mustered a nod.

"All right, then," Amna said quietly. Her eyes flicked over to the door. No one was listening. Not even Bloodbath.

"Teresa's not one of the wildfolk," she began. "She was born here."

That made him turn his head toward her. That made his eyelids raise a little higher. "In Petrossia?" he croaked.

"In the *Winter Palace*," she said, and he could hear how

pleased she was that her story was helping him stand firm and fight the defeat seeping into him.

Pieter let out a huff and turned away on his side. "You're lying again," he said. "No one's born here."

"Alexander was," said Amna.

"Yeah," Pieter said with a snort, "but he's *royalty*. . . ."

Suddenly he was awake. Suddenly he was sitting up. Suddenly he was staring. Amnabushka looked back at him with wide, unblinking eyes.

"Yes, Alexander is royalty," she said. "He's also Teresa's brother."

4

The Tale of Teresa Gust

In all the Hall of Faces, there was not one picture of a queen. Not one single czarina. All down the wide wall, in every gilded picture frame, the Iron Crown of Petrossia sat on a king's head. It had passed from father to first-born son for a thousand years.

This explains why the Empire was such a dreadful place.

It also explains why, when Princess Teresa Augusta Fabergé the First (to give Teresa her full name) was ten minutes old, she was already being lowered down the chimney.

"You better be a boy," the Czar told the bump.

The Czarina looked down at her belly. "Why must she?"

"*He*, my love," corrected the Czar. "Why must *he*. Because girls are weak, and boys are strong. I must have a son to wear my crown."

The Czarina laughed at her husband's nonsense. How

could girls be weak, when she herself was the greatest warrior in Petrossia? Had she not been the one who had come across the Boreal Sea from Albion, and surprised the Czar during the Yuletide feast, and—with nothing but her smile—conquered the hidden kingdom of his heart?

"Perhaps my love is right," said the Czar, glancing nervously around at his War Council behind him. He was a younger king back in those days, not yet turned cruel by his crown and conquests. "What does it matter if *he* comes out, and he has decided to be a *she*?"

But his War Council all frowned, and the Warmaster yanked his knotted beard to show his anger.

"Czars have *sons*," said Ugor. "Not puny daughters."

"It is a tradition not even alchemy can change," said Alchemaster Blüstav. "It will be hard for you to keep your crown unless you have a son for an heir."

"Do not worry, Sire," said Lord Xin with sickly sweetness. "When the baby comes to be born, I am sure Her Majesty the Czarina will take care of everything." He smiled his dark smile. "Or we will have to."

Now the Czarina was no longer laughing. It was not the Czar she was afraid of. She knew her husband's temper long before she had decided to make him marry her. He was like a spring storm—all bluster and howls, but with her, his raging never lasted. Soon he would be all soppy again, his fragile smile appearing from beneath his mustache like the Bloom sun from behind a cloud.

These men, though, were different. Their hearts were ugly swamps she would not want to conquer even if she could, and they were as cold and cruel as this country's winter.

The Czarina did not know what they might do to her daughter, for it *was* a daughter she carried and not a son. Her handmaid Amnabushka had told her so. It was Amna who had read the freckles on the back of the Czarina's hand, and sang them the magic song until they moved across the skin and made the shape of the hieroglyph for girl-child.

"Amnabushka," she said, summoning her handmaid once the War Council had left her chambers. "What can I do?"

Amna touched the wooden key tied into her hair, as if it might unlock the answer. Then suddenly, she spoke: "There is a way, my Patra. Not an easy one. A hard path, both for you and the child."

The Czarina gripped Amna's hand tight. "Tell me."

That night, Amnabushka put on her peekaboo, left the Royal Chamber, and headed down to the kitchens. There amongst the shelves, she searched the crates until she found the vials of food dyes. They glinted on the rack, arranged from blood-red to deep-sea blue, and every shade of color in between, like a rainbow divided up and bottled.

Amna picked a blue the color of starlight, and a shade of moon white. Then she stole away a saucepan from a hook above the stoves, and hurried back upstairs to the Czarina.

A week later the bump stirred, and decided to be born.

Whilst the Czar paced anxiously back and forth outside the Royal Chambers, waiting to meet his son, the Czarina said good-bye to the daughter she cradled in her arms. She kissed her baby's little forehead. Teresa snuffled in her sleep.

"My Patra," her handmaid whispered. "We must hurry."

The Czarina bent her head, and her tears rolled down her chin and dropped on the cheeks of her daughter. Teresa woke from her first sleep, blinking those wide green eyes—the eyes of her father.

"My Patra," said Amna again. "It has to be now. If the men come in and see her . . ."

She did not have to say it. The Czarina knew that she must break her own heart so that Teresa's might have a chance to keep on beating. And so she let her handmaid lift the baby away, and take Teresa to the ashen fireplace, where the grapple lay winched to a saucepan.

Before Amna put the lid on, she unscrewed the bottle of colorings and raised up the pipette. One drop, two drops squeezed and fell like tears. Teresa scrunched up her face and started to wail. Her eyes were green no longer—now they were the color of starlight. The crown of her head was lathered in the moon white, until Teresa's hair was the same as Amna's. Now the princess had become a wildfolk slave.

Amnabushka murmured the saying, said to all Baba

Sisters: *"Many miles may you live."* Then, quickly, before the men heard the crying, Amna put the saucepan lid on. Taking up the rope, she lowered Petrossia's true heir down into the kitchens.

"She will be safe, my Patra," Amna said. "I will see to it. Dry those eyes. Despair not. A day will come when she will rise out of the kitchens, and come seeking her mama true."

The Czarina did not reply. She sat looking down at her arms, where Teresa had lain in all her lightness.

"Prepare the room," she said at last. "Inform the Czar of the tragedy."

Amna moved to draw the curtains, and dim the room. Out from the wardrobe, she took the black mourning dresses.

By the banks of the Ossia, they buried a casket full of stones. It was said amongst the Petrossia folk that the Czarina's joy had died along with her child, and it was true that her smile—the greatest weapon in all the land—was after that time like a sword set in stone that no one could draw out.

She could no longer bring herself to love the Czar. To her, he was not the strongest of men, but the weakest. If he were truly mighty, he would not care for old and foolish traditions. He would not have lost a daughter for want of a son. He would not have broken his wife's heart for want of an heir.

The Czarina, in her sadness and anger, began to rule the kingdom of the Czar's heart with careless neglect, not caring if she was queen there or not, and so she did not notice the darker, crueler love creeping in to replace her: the love of conquering.

She even began to encourage the Czar to march off with his armies on one of his wars, longing for the times he was away battling in far-off lands. For when that happened, the Czarina was alone in the Royal Chamber. Then, she could throw a grapple down the flue and winch Teresa up from the kitchens.

Out of the chimney the saucepan would come, with starry-eyed Teresa appearing in the darkness. Mother and daughter. Daughter and mother. Looking at each other with love and with wonder.

For a few precious hours, everything would be happy again. Teresa and her mother would laugh in whispers, and sing in almost-silence, and happiness would swell inside them both—as light as bubbles, and as quick to burst. The Czarina's famous smile shone from her face once again, and Teresa's smile (fiercer than her mother's, and more mischievous) beamed back.

But this could only happen if the kitchen cooks weren't

watching, and if the hearth wasn't lit, and if it was the dead of night and there was no risk of being discovered. Long weeks passed in which Teresa and the Czarina could not even see each other once. In those times, the Czarina felt like she was dying of thirst, and only the sight of Teresa coming up the chimney—like a bucket of cold clear water drawn from a well—could end the drought in her heart.

Time passed. Teresa outgrew first the saucepan, then the stew pot, then the gravy keg that she traveled up the chimney in.

"How big you're getting," the Czarina said one night as they sat together.

"You're big too, Mama," Teresa said, poking her belly.

"One day," said the Czarina, "there won't be a pot big enough to hold you."

"I'll climb then, Mama. I'm doing good practice on the shelves. I do good gathering. Amna calls me Little Monkey. Look." Teresa stuffed a fist into her pocket, then brought out a few sprigs from the herb garden: dill, pepperleaf, mintflower.

"You fetched them all yourself?" The Czarina bunched them up like a bouquet of flowers, and kissed Teresa on the nose. Teresa beamed and threw her arms around her mother. Then she reared back.

"Mama!" she said. "Your big belly just poked me!"

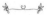

The Czarina turned pink. "That's your baby brother, Teresa."

Teresa blinked her wide eyes. "A baby's hiding in *there*?" She knocked on the belly as if it were a door, then wrinkled her nose when there was no reply. "Why doesn't he come out and play with us?"

"In a little while, he will," said the Czarina. "But when he does, he won't be able to play with us for long, Teresa."

Teresa thought about this. "Because I'm secret, and he might tell about me?"

The Czarina nodded. "He might."

"Babies can't keep good secrets, can they, Mama? They go blah-blah-blah."

"Yes, they do."

"Especially boys," said Teresa, voice full of pity. "Boys can't even help it." Her face lit up with a sudden idea. "Maybe he might be a girl instead?"

The Czarina looked very sad then. "No, Teresa. Amna has sung her song again, and I have seen what the freckles say. You will have a brother."

She gripped Teresa tight, and hugged her hard.

"He will have a hard life, Teresa. As hard as yours, but in a different way. Promise me, when your little brother is older, that you will be his friend."

Teresa cocked her head like a sparrow. "Will he be nice to me?"

"I think he will," the Czarina said softly, cradling her belly with her hand. "I think he will be nice to everyone. That is why he will need your help. Do you promise me that you will look after him?"

Teresa promised.

Three nights later, Alexander arrived too soon.

The birth made Mama sick. She kept to her bed, while Amna took her temperature and read the thermometer with worried looks.

Teresa began climbing up the chimney herself, for Mama no longer had the strength to winch the gravy keg up from the kitchen. She brought mintflowers from the kitchen shelves, so Mama's bedside would always smell of Bloom, her favorite month. Mama stayed tucked up, pale and shivery, listening to Teresa's talk of spices and shelf exploring.

Sometimes little Alexander was with her, and Teresa would sit and hold his little pink hand with her fingers. His mouth was all smiles, his eyes were all gentleness, his hair was all curls and his cheeks were all pudge. Teresa loved him, fierce and hot as a flame.

Then, one day, Alexander was gone. The Czar had

decided he no longer needed mothering. It was time he learned to conquer with the Heirmaster. Lord Xin had taken the prince away, to teach Alexander how to swing his tiny rattle (which was spiked, like a bommy-knocker).

Alexander's absence only made Mama sadder, and sicker. All through Welkin, Worsen, and Yule, her blankets grew stiff with the cold. Her room would glitter with frost, as if it were strewn with diamonds, but she refused to light the hearth and miss a visit from her daughter.

"You're all the warmth I need," she'd tell Teresa.

But a fire was going out in the Czarina. Sadness seeped into her like damp seeps into wood. Teresa bought her khave spiced with blazing pip, and bouquets of poppyweed, with flowers red as flames. But nothing could rekindle her long-gone smile. She died on the first day of spring. Life just drifted away from her, the way wind blows blossoms from a tree.

When the Czar returned from his latest victory to find his queen was dead, he rode his army straight to the River Ossia. Two hundred horses hauled a passing iceberg from the water and heaved it to the Winter Palace graveyards. Using Viktor, the Czar hacked and hollowed it out, turning it into a building of ice that became known as the Chapel of the Frozen Tear.

It was said by those who saw him that His Majesty wept whilst he worked, like he was part of the Fountain of Sobs. It was said by the time he was done, an icicle of tears hung from his chin in the bitter cold. And finally it was said that the Czar had cried his whole life's worth of tears in that moment, that his kindness had died along with his love, and forever afterward his heart knew no sorrow, nor remorse, nor love, nor mercy.

Inside the chapel, he lay the Czarina in her coffin of æther and ice. Although it was forbidden for anyone but the royal family to enter and gaze upon her frozen beauty, every week for years afterward the guards would find small bunches of mintflower placed upon her grave. No one knew who kept putting them there, and how, or when, or why.

5

A Grim Encounter

"So that's how it all began," Amnabushka said in the silence after her story.

"Why didn't she tell me?" Pieter wondered. "Did she not trust me?"

"Many and many a reason," said Amna. "None to do with you. Shame, that she was the daughter of such a tyrant. Guilt, that his wickedness was somehow her fault. And last of all, fear."

"Of the Czar?"

Amna shook her head. "Not of him. Of herself."

Pieter slumped his shoulders. "I don't understand."

Amna's smile was small and sad. "Of course you don't. But if you had a father that became a monster, wouldn't you be afraid of becoming just like him?"

Pieter closed his eyes. "It's all so sad. All so hopeless."

"Tallymaster!" Amna thumped the ground by his head.

"Didn't you listen to the story? The Czarina despaired, and look what happened to her!"

"You should have told a fairy tale," Pieter mumbled. "You should have told a story . . . where people live . . . happily ever after . . ."

"I will!" Amna shook his shoulders, like he was having a nightmare he couldn't wake from. "Listen! Bloom and Swoon and many a moon ago . . ."

But Pieter was already snoring.

This time he wouldn't wake, no matter how hard Amna elbowed him.

Pieter had lost heart. Crumbled. Given up. Succumbed. He drifted off to sleep and waved a white flag in his dreams. The flag became a rag, became a tatter, did not even matter. All color bleached away. His dreams turned gray, then faded to black. Wrong collapsed into right. Day bled into night. Time slipped away.

Pieter tumbled down a long steep slope toward a place of no hope. . . .

And then—at the end of everything—he woke.

Hello! a voice said. **Please vacate your body!**

Pieter felt light. Empty. Like a bubble must feel before it pops. Was this a dream? Strange. He thought he'd given dreams up. His sleep had been one long stretch of darkness.

The voice spoke again, echoing inside his head: **Welcome to the Afterlife!**

Pieter remembered the voice, and suddenly he saw who it belonged to.

A black-robed skeleton was gliding across the carpet toward him.

It seemed to be carrying a scythe.

I'm Grim, the skeleton said. **Though you may know me as the Pale Traveler.** Within the two empty eye sockets, two round pupils were glowing like tinderfly eggs. **Now that you're dead, it's my job to get you from Life to Death. Here, boy. Come here.**

Dread—cold and heavy as a tombstone slab—lay heavy on Pieter. He had surrendered almost everything in the Gloom Room, but he had not yet given up on fear.

"This is a dream," he whispered.

At the sound of his breath, Grim's head swiveled down on its spine. His pupils turned a light pink color. **Oh**, he said. **You can see me? I actually wasn't talking to you.**

From the sleeve of his robe, he extended five bone fingers, long and white as pianola keys, and gave Bloodbath's tail a yank. There was a sound like a page being torn out of a book. *Rip!* The skeleton pulled up a thin see-through thing from the poodle, like a blue and sparkly petal.

With a sharp gasp, Pieter realized that it was Bloodbath's *soul.*

Down on the carpet, the poor dog's body slumped lifeless to the ground. Bloodbath had been whipped away from his body in the same way a magician might whip a tablecloth off a dinner table without even wobbling the wine glasses.

Very sorry for the confusion, Grim said to Pieter. **You'll have to wait a little longer. You see, you're not actually dead yet. Just having a Near-Death Experience. Unlike Bloodbath here.**

Grim turned back to the poodle, and grinned. It was his default facial expression.

Here, boy! This way! he said cheerfully to Bloodbath. **Unless you'd like to put in a request for a haunting.**

Bloodbath barked.

The Czar? said Grim as he walked off with the soul of the poodle trotting beside him. **That's understandable. I get a *lot* of requests for him. There's a waiting list, you understand? It's several decades long. Let me put your name down . . .**

As soon as Grim had gone, Pieter drifted back to sleep. He did not think how close he had just come to Death, nor did he care that the Pale Traveler might be coming back for him. He did not think anything at all. He was totally empty, like a paper bag blowing in the wind. That's what surrender was like.

He floated through his dreams, waiting for Grim to come back.

But before Death came to take Pieter from the Gloom Room, someone else did.

"Wake up, Tallymaster."

From very far away, Pieter heard Ugor's voice. Then a sausage-thick finger flicked him, hard. The nail left a pain in Pieter's cheek like a bee sting.

"What's going on?" he said, struggling up onto his elbows and looking around with bleary eyes. He was no longer in the Gloom Room—Ugor had carried him out into the corridor. The dreadful despair it had filled him with was gone.

The Warmaster towered over him, wearing a Father Frost outfit of blue velvet, trimmed with reindeer fur. His injured eye had healed and he had regrown his beard. It was whitened with flour, with a silver bell tied to the end. If you were awake to hear Father Frost's bell ring, it was said you would get no presents.

"Happy Yuletide," said the Warmaster, yanking Pieter to his feet. "Up. Need you. Now."

"Whatever it is, get your elves to do it," said Pieter.

(It was his first joke in months. He was a little out of practice.)

"Ho, ho, ho," growled Ugor. "Very funny. Come to Hall of Faces. *Quick*."

"What's all the panic about?" Pieter asked. "Did someone forget to leave carrots out for Rudolf?"

(All right, *very* out of practice.)

"What about Amna?" Pieter asked. "What about Bloodbath?"

"Sweep still prisoner," Ugor answered. "Poodle die, though."

Pieter remembered his strange dream of the skeleton that took Bloodbath's soul, and shivered. Perhaps it hadn't been a dream at all.

"Where are we going?" he said.

"Czar not wake from Hall of Faces this morn," said Ugor. "Door still locked from inside. No answer. Maybe Prince disobeying His Majesty again. I show him you. Then he behave again." Ugor's bear paw of a hand tightened, and Pieter winced. "Or Ugor pull you like cracker, make you go snap."

Pieter said nothing more as he hurried him down the halls, but his heart was running faster than their footsteps.

Because there was another reason to explain why the Czar could not be woken.

"Operation: *His Royal Whiskers*," he said under his breath.

Could it be? Could *Teresa* have come back down the chimney last night, just like Father Frost, bringing the Czar the only present he deserved?

Pieter hoped so. It was not a foolish hope either. Because if Yuletide promised one thing, it was that every winter, no matter how long and terrible, did one day come to an end.

6

An Even Grimmer Encounter

They passed through hallways decorated with iron tinsel and bright red baubles that hung from the ceiling like frozen drops of blood. Everpine trees filled each room with their fresh forest scent. Tinderflies burned on toffee candles. Butlers and maids hurried past, carefully carrying presents (mostly crossbow shaped) and samovars of mull, the Yuletide sweet wine.

That afternoon, soldiers and Petrossia folk from all across the Empire would gather in the Winter Palace courtyard to celebrate the start of another year of conquering. The War Council would march at the head of the finest of the Czar's army, the crowds would cheer, and everyone would feast to the glory of Petrossia. (Although this year, because of Alexander's appetite, it would be less like a feast, and more like a light starter of beetroot soup and butterless bread.)

At last, they came to the corridor that led to the Hall of Faces. Two guards stood by the doorway with sprigs of mistletoe tied to their spears. They unpuckered their lips quickly when they saw it was Ugor stomping toward them.

The Warmaster rapped his knuckles on the stained glass, and at once, a Slinja unfolded out at them from his hiding place inside the keyhole.

"Still no sign of the Czar, Warmaster," said the Slinja in his raspy voice. "His Majesty must still be sleeping in the prince's fur as usual. His Highness Alexander has not woken, either. All is well."

The barbarian scratched his forehead. "Too late for sleeping in. Something wrong."

The Slinja shook his head, which had the effect of making it disappear and reappear several times. "Impossible. No one has been in or out of the hall since last night."

Ugor's eyes narrowed. "Wakey-wakey time then. Open the door."

"Yes, Warmaster." Quick as a flash, the Slinja folded up, poked himself through the keyhole and disappeared from sight. Ugor grabbed Pieter up by the scruff of his shirt and tucked him under his arm.

"You come too," he said. "If Alexander hurt Czar, Ugor hurt *you*."

Pieter didn't reply. He just focused on trying not to gag. Father Frost was supposed to live up in the Waste, and conduct the Aurora lights with an icicle baton. He was supposed to smell of æther and pine needles, not old sweat and bacon grease.

The lock clicked, the handle twitched, and the heavy doors began to swing slowly open. Pieter held his breath, and not just because of Ugor's stink. What had happened in the Hall of Faces? And who would he see?

There was just Alexander, filling the hall with his size and his snores.

Pieter let out a disappointed sigh. If the prince hadn't even woken up yet, there was no way Teresa had come, overthrown the Czar, and changed him into a kitten.

"Your Majesty?" said the Warmaster. The barbarian's voice echoed across the hall. "Sire?" he said a little louder.

One huge green eye, flecked with brown and gold and irritation, opened just a little, then slumped closed.

"Young Majesty!" Ugor rang the bell on his beard. "Yuletide!"

"Now he *definitely* won't open his eyes," said Pieter to the barbarian. "If you hear Father Frost's bell, you're supposed to be asleep."

"Shut it," snapped the Warmaster, his swine breath blasting

Pieter in the face. He stomped over to Alexander's ear and roared: "TEN OF THE MORN! HIS MAJESTY THE CZAR AND HIS YOUNG MAJESTY THE PRINCE NEED—"

Alexander held up a paw. Five claws slid out, like swords from their scabbards.

"—To go sleep as long as they want," finished Ugor, holding up his hands and backing away. "Pardon Ugor, Ugor knows how Young Majesty wuvs his snoozie-woozies."

Pieter couldn't help grinning as Alexander's claws retracted, his paw slumped over his ears, and his snoring continued.

"Young Majesty can sleep," Ugor muttered. "But Czar must wake before Yuletide feast."

Behind a pillar was a ladder that Amna had once used to dust the portraits. Ugor fetched it, and placed it against the prince's belly. It stretched high up into Alexander's golden fur. There was a snapping sound, like a pulled cracker, when he stepped onto it. The Warmaster looked down at the first rung, broken under his boot. Then he looked at his huge gut. Then he looked at Pieter.

"Ugor too heavy!" he said, slinging Pieter up onto the ladder. "Go wake Czar!"

Anything was better than being tucked under a barbarian

armpit. What choice did Pieter have, anyway? He climbed a rung, and then another. The Czar was nowhere to be found. He looked down at Ugor and shrugged. The Warmaster glared back, and motioned for him to go farther up.

Soon Pieter had run out of ladder to climb. Ugor was far below. Carefully, heart hammering in his chest, he stepped onto Alexander. The prince's fur was light and warm, and came up to his waist. It made a soft, swishing sound as he waded through it, like ripe corn. The ceiling was just above his head, so close he could reach up and touch the iron tinsel hanging from the chandeliers.

Square-rooting his fear, he wandered up Alexander's back, toward his head. With each step, the prince's chest rose and fell—it was like walking in a meadow and on a bouncy castle at the same time. It was another world, up here. He had never felt so small, or so alone.

Ahead, there was a patch of hair different from the rest. It was flattened down. Pieter knew that it was where the Czar lay sleeping. Why hadn't Ugor's roar been enough to wake him? He stepped closer, and saw the reason.

The Czar, broad as a bear, strong as an ox, hairy as a goat, was lying there in his armor and boots and cape.

And he was dead.

It took Pieter a moment to realize it. At first glance, the Czar had not been stabbed, shot, or blown up. His armor was not broken, his Iron Crown still lay on his head, and his face looked strangely peaceful. Yet his deathly white skin hung loosely from his body like empty silk pajamas.

With a sick feeling in his stomach, Pieter saw that every last drop of the Czar's blood had been drained. There were two holes at his neck, like bite marks.

The Czar was not just dead—he had been murdered.

Pieter was not good with gruesomeness. He reeled away, queasy and faint and suddenly frightened. Alexander's fur was swaying and rustling around him, but there was no breeze in the hall. At that moment he knew for sure that he was not alone. *No one has been in or out*, the Slinja bodyguard had said. The murderer who had done away with the greatest conqueror of all time was still there, hidden in the prince's hair.

Something touched Pieter's leg, and he yelled out. Dark clouds of spots flashed in front of his eyes. He threw up his hands in terror, hearing sharp cracks, and the clatter of broken glass from over by the doors. Far below, Ugor grunted in surprise.

Pieter stumbled away and ran, until his stomach gave a lurch and the rustling ginger meadow sloped into a narrow cliff. With a stifled shriek he slid and swerved down the helter-skelter slope of Alexander's curled-up tail, rolled across the floor, and finally jerked to a stop when he collided with Ugor's boots.

Alexander fidgeted in his sleep, and a few moments later, the husk of the Czar's body fell to the ground beside Pieter, as brittle and lifeless as an autumn leaf.

The Warmaster's eyes swiveled from the Czar's body to Pieter, and back again.

"Who?" Ugor cried. "Who did this?"

Pieter had no idea who had killed the Czar, and his genius brain was still spinning in his skull, too dizzy to work it out.

Which meant Ugor found his own answer. This was unfortunate, as the barbarian was not on the War Council for his intelligence. While Pieter lay there, not really thinking about anything except how important it was not to puke, the Warmaster conducted his own investigation, using mainly the process of elimination.

"Not Alexander," he said slowly. "Not *me*. Not Slinja still guarding door."

He looked around for other suspects.

There was no one else in the Hall but Pieter.

Pieter should have taken that moment to point out a number of important clues that Ugor had overlooked. One:

he was a puny boy with no weapon. Two: he was not a vampyr. Three: the Czar was cold as a stone, meaning the murder had obviously happened hours ago.

Unfortunately, before Pieter realized that he was Ugor's prime suspect, he had reached another conclusion: he was going to be sick. By the time he'd finished puking over the Warmaster's boots, Ugor had already arrested him for the murder of the Czar, and sentenced Pieter to death.

Alexander, meanwhile, snoozed on.

Unaware that he was now the Empurrer of all Petrossia.

Unaware that his father had been killed.

Unaware his joint-best friend was about to suffer the same fate.

PART FOUR
Yuletide

. . . on the pedestal, these words appear:
"My name is Ozymandias, King of Kings;
Look on my Works, ye Mighty, and despair!"
Nothing beside remains. Round the decay
Of that colossal wreck, boundless and bare
The lone and level sands stretch far away.

—"OZYMANDIAS," PERCY SHELLEY

Whereabouts is your death, O Koschei?

—*THE DEATH OF KOSCHEI THE DEATHLESS*,
RUSSIAN FAIRY TALE

1

The Coronation of Empurrer Alexander

The rest of the War Council quickly scheduled Pieter's execution to be the highlight of the Yuletide feast. First, the crowds were to gather and toast the memory of the Czar as he was put to rest; then Prince Alexander would be crowned as Empurrer; and finally Petrossia's traitorous, murderous Tallymaster would receive his just desserts.

Trapped up in his tallychamber, where he could be quickly fetched for execution, Pieter counted three ways to stop his imminent beheading. Either Alexander had to wake up, or Teresa had to come back, or he had to solve the mystery of who had murdered the Czar.

Pieter was mathemagically certain that one of those things would happen in the next few hours. As news of the Czar's death had spread through the palace, Amna had escaped from the Gloom Room in all the chaos, and gone to hide in the aviary. She was there right now, madly scribbling the same message over and over, tying it to the foot of every pigeon and releasing it from its cage. One of them had come to Pieter's window, letting him read what Amna was writing.

Teresa Gust
Come home quick
Pieter in peril

Maybe Teresa was somewhere far away—in Albion perhaps—and news of the Czar's death would take a long time to reach her. Even if that was true, Alexander was now the Empurrer of all Petrossia. As soon as he woke, he would surely decree that Pieter's life must be spared.

But, just in case Alexander snoozed on through the day (like kittens have a habit of doing), or Amna's pigeons were all shot from the sky and cooked in Yuletide pies, Pieter's brain was hard at work solving the mystery that could save his life.

If he hadn't murdered the Czar, then who had?

When he thought of all the facts, Pieter was certain that the murderer had to have been in the room with the Czar and Alexander when the doors were closed the evening before. The Slinjas had kept constant watch all night, and nothing had entered in or out of the hall, except for Pieter and Ugor.

Which then begged the question: why had the Slinjas (or the Czar, or Pieter himself for that matter) not seen the killer?

Sir Klaus could have snuck past the bodyguards. But even the Spymaster could not have squeezed through the locked door.

Maybe it was an assassin: when Pieter had seen the black spots springing across his vision, a panel of stained-glass door at the far corner of the room had shattered.

Bullet holes, perhaps?

No, that couldn't be, his brain decided. *You would have heard the gun as it fired.*

But what if the assassin had used a singing pistol?

Then where were the bullets? came the answer. *And besides, bullets cannot suck every drop of blood from your veins. Where was the blood?*

Again and again, Pieter went over the facts he could not draw together into a solution: broken glass; black spots in the prince's fur; an invisible killer; the two holes at the Czar's neck; his body, drained of blood.

It was the perfect locked-room murder. The doors were guarded, there were no windows, and the chimney had been blocked up since Teresa's escape.

What was the solution? Who did it? How?

But to these questions, Pieter's brain had no answer. Not at eleven of the morn, nor at noon when the orkestar in the courtyard raised their instruments and began to play a funeral dirge.

Many kings and queens of the third continent spend their whole lives building their tombs: enormous pyramids and opulent mausoleums that last a thousand lifetimes and grant their own peculiar form of immortality.

Princess Josefin of Laplönd was building herself a crypt completely out of diamonds. The Duke of Madri was planning to have himself dipped in a molten vat of gold (along with his new poodle, Grisly) and periodically taken to parties by his remaining servants, so that he would not miss out on the latest gossip.

The Czar was not like any of these rulers. He had never built himself a tomb, because he was far more concerned with the deaths of his enemies than his own demise. (And it had always been his ultimate ambition to conquer Death before he came to die.)

Now there was nowhere to put his dried-out remains. No grave could be dug—the winter ground was as hard as iron. He ended up being wrapped up in some leftover polka-dot wrapping paper and burned on a bed of chopped-up everpine.

The funeral was quick. The fire was fierce. The crowd was silent. Only Warmaster Ugor, dressed as Father Frost, sobbed tears that dripped down into his whitened beard and turned it into a hairy icicle. The stringalins played a final note, bringing to an end both the Czar's reign and the winter, which, as far as winters and reigns go, had been the most terrible in all of Petrossian history.

So far.

Things were about to get worse—a lot worse.

Especially for Pieter.

Next came the coronation in the grounds outside the Hall of Faces. Petrossia's greatest soldiers had oiled their muskets, sharpened their spears, and polished their shields. Now they marched into the courtyard, column after column of them, led by the War Council, while the Petrossia folk stood on either side and looked on in fear and awe.

What a fearsome collection of fighters had gathered there! Hundreds of ranks! Dozens of columns! The finest warriors from all one hundred armies, all standing in silent attention and awaiting their new ruler!

Lord Xin arrived on Artifax, his bird the size of an ostrich that could run as fast as the wind. Behind him, marched the Cossack Cavalry, Tartar Musketmen, and Mongol Archers.

Ugor had come with Onk-Onk, his armored pig that fired bullets from its snout. He rode at the head of Vikings riding bears and Saracens riding camels.

One after the other, they all trooped in and stood rigidly at attention by the vast cat-flap door to the Hall of Faces, until finally Alexander appeared from within.

Up in his tallychamber, Pieter felt the tremor of his friend's footsteps. Down below, the crowds of Petrossia folk edged back from the door. Even some of the spears held by the soldiers started to shake. The great door creaked and swung. Out came the enormous kitten, as tall as the Winter Palace itself.

And his green eyes were filled with lonely grief. In them, Pieter could see the sweet little boy, still only six years old, who had just woken up late this Yuletide morn to find that his father was dead. Not a good father, but still his father, the only one he'd ever had, and would never have again.

Perhaps it might seem strange that Alexander might mourn the Czar. His father had despised and bullied him all his life, then tried to kill his friends. But that is the nature of love: it is given regardless of whether it is deserved. And if there was one thing the prince had learned since his sixth birthday, it was that people could change. If a little boy could become a gigantic kitten, then perhaps it was not so foolish for Alexander to have hoped that his father might one day have loved him.

"Alexander! I'm up here! They're going to execute me!" Pieter yelled and thumped on his locked window, but his cries were drowned out. At the War Council's bidding, a great cheer went up from the soldiers. A gilded pulley winched up a golden crown bigger than a carriage wheel onto Alexander's head, while the Iron Crown was slipped like a ring over the tip of one claw.

"Look up!" Pieter cried, waving and yelling in his room until he was exhausted. "Alexander, please! Look up and save me!"

But Alexander's head stayed bowed, weighed down by the weight of his crown and his heartache.

In contrast, the barbarians and the Tartars and the Mongols and the Cossacks all looked perfectly happy. The Czar might be dead, but his son was an unstoppable avalanche of ginger fur and claws. Surely he would lead them to new and glorious conquests! They would subjugate the rest of the Earth, then the Moon, then fulfill the Czar's ultimate ambition and conquer Death itself!

"Happy Yuletide and Coronation, Empurrer Alexander!" cried Lord Xin, his voice ringing out across the square. "The troops seek glorious battle once more in your honor! Tell us! Tomorrow will be the first day of Bloom, and in the coming weeks the weather will be warm enough for our armies to march forth. Which country shall we conquer in the spring? Do we cross the Boreal Sea and invade Albion? Do we march through the Woodn't to Hertz?"

Emperor Alexander flicked out a paw and scratched his answer into the courtyard cobblestones. Lord Xin eagerly craned his neck forward to read it, then frowned.

"Ah, Your Majesty," he said quietly. "We have actually already conquered the Kingdom of Hungary."

Alexander slumped his shoulders and wrote a second word beside his first. And once again, the Heirmaster bit his lip and muttered, "Sire, Turkey too is also part of Your Empire."

The Mongol horses stamped. The barbarians snorted and pulled at their beards. Lord Xin looked uneasily at Alexander, wondering what was wrong. He had tutored Alexander himself—the prince was not a fool, he had known which kingdoms and countries he was to inherit.

Now he was Empurrer, had he suddenly forgotten?

With obvious frustration, Alexander wrote a third word.

"Roast chicken?!" said the Heirmaster in bewilderment. "Where in the world is the *Kingdom of Roast Chicken*?!"

And then with a horrified gasp, he understood.

So did Pieter, watching from the tallychamber window.

Alexander wasn't giving orders for battle—he was asking to be cheered up with food. Just like when he had been sad on his birthday, and Pieter and Teresa had made him a cake.

At once, Ugor dismissed the now grumbling armies and prepared the crowds for the feast and execution. On the way out, the Mongols and Tartars began to argue over who should march through the gates first, and the Cossacks glared darkly at their Empurrer and made disgruntled mutterings under their breath.

Pieter gulped. It looked like the list of traitors that lay somewhere in his tallychamber was going to need updating very soon.

(A NOTE ON LOYALTY)

It was perhaps not surprising that most of the Czar's hundred armies followed him out of fear, not love. They did not fight for Petrossia because they loved the people who lived there, or were proud of its culture and language, or enjoyed its national dish (six shots of vodka and a barrel of beetroot soup), or were obsessed with its national sport (the rules of which have long been forgotten, but involve a bag of greased ferrets).

The Czar's armies fought for him because he *won*.

And now that he was gone, they looked restless.

2

Things Go from Gory to Ghoulish

Pieter could scarcely believe what was happening.

Over the course of one spectacularly dreadful Yuletide day, everything had changed. It looked like Petrossia was going the way of winter—with the Czar gone, the great frozen empire he had smothered over the land like a glacier felt like it might melt away to nothing. It was as if an astonishing alchemical experiment had started on Yuletide morn, and was transforming the entire country.

Was this somehow Teresa's doing? Pieter thought it must be, and his heart swelled with a joy he thought he had left locked away in the Gloom Room. But at the same time, he was aware of another enormous change that was about to happen: in a few hours' time, he would be without his head.

"There must be a way out of this," he told his genius brain. "Think! Think!"

Stop thinking at me! his brain snapped back. *You're taking up valuable head space!*

So Pieter just sat in his miserable tallychamber, trying to square-root his ever-increasing fear, while the crowds below ate their miserable coronation feast of beetroot soup and butterless bread.

He was still there at three of the afternoon, when the executioner came to fetch him.

There were plenty of executioners in Petrossia. During the Czar's reign, it had been a lucrative business (His Majesty had loved a good beheading, and even performed several himself). But over the years, so many heads had been lopped off, chopped off, and sliced off, that the crowds had begun to get bored.

In an attempt to make it more exciting, executioners had started to remove their victims' heads in ever more imaginative ways. And as the echoing footsteps came up the spiral stairs, Pieter wondered who might be coming to execute him, and how.

Was it the Guillotiger, who wore the red velvet jacket and black silk hat of a circus showman, and made you kneel between the jaws of his tiger, which then bit your head off in one chomp?

Perhaps it was Uncorkula, the enormously tall and thin vampyr with skin the color of moonlight, who shook you like a champagne bottle, gave you a single sharp twist, uncorked your head from your shoulders, then poured out a pint of your blood into a crystal champagne flute and drank it?

Or maybe it was—most horrifying of all—the Spoonatic, a crazy old babushka who executed people using nothing but a rusty dessert spoon?[21]

Pieter was trembling and his belly was quaking and—worst of all—his brain was blank as the executioner opened the door to the tallychamber.

It wasn't the Guillotiger.

Nor Uncorkula nor the Spoonatic.

"*Bonjour*, and Happy Yuletide," said the executioner. "I am Monsieur Snippy."

Monsieur Snippy had a thick Praisian accent. It was like he spoke with a mouthful of cream. He wore cherry red shoes with a turquoise suit made of silk brocade, hemmed with white frills. His face was powdered, with a black beauty spot, and enormously thick white eyebrows plucked into the silhouettes of two swans. He wore a tall lilac wig, woven into the shape of a pair of scissors.

"You must be Pieter," said Monsieur Snippy, holding his

---

21. You may be wondering how you execute someone with a rusty dessert spoon. Very slowly, is the answer. That's why the Spoonatic was so terrifying.

hand out for Pieter to shake. His fingers were slender, with long nails, and painted on each one was a miniature version of a famous portrait.

"Let's get to work!" said the monsieur, stepping inside the tallychamber. He clicked his fingers and Ugor came in carrying a dainty table with an oval mirror, and a red velvet seat. "Put it by the window, please, Warmaster. It's dim in here, but we will have to make do. Take a seat, take a seat."

Pieter was ushered into the chair. Monsieur Snippy swiveled him around to face the mirror and Pieter saw his own startled reflection staring back at him. To his surprise, he was smiling. Suddenly he realized why. Death at the hands of Monsieur Snippy would be nowhere near as gruesome as the Guillotiger or Uncorkula, nor as lengthy as the Spoonatic. As executions go, this would be quite a pleasant one.

(He could not have been more wrong. In fact, no genius had ever thought something so spectacularly incorrect.)

"Don't worry, Pieter," Monsieur Snippy said. "I've done this a thousand times, you're in very safe hands."

Before he knew what was happening, the monsieur had pulled a hidden lever, and leather straps buckled themselves tight around Pieter's arms and legs. He was utterly trapped. Then, pulling open the drawers of his table, Monsieur

Snippy took out various wigs, powders, lipsticks, mascara, and glitter pouches.

And while his victim sat helplessly, the executioner set to work.

He rouged Pieter's cheeks, plumped his lips, plucked his eyebrows, fitted him with pink sunglasses, glued on a false mustache, added clip-on chandelier earrings, stuck a crystal beauty spot on his cheek, added liner to his eyelids and nostrils, defined his cheekbones, gave him a prosthetic chin that looked like a tiny bottom, hung tiny rainbow-colored bells on his eyelashes, added two fake sapphire tears to the corners of his eyes, whitened his teeth, and dabbed glitter on his forehead. All the while, he shouted out enthusiastic phrases like:

"Let's get you from drab to fab!"

"Executions are ten percent beheading, ninety percent *showbiz*!"

"If you're going to die for crime, might as well look divine!"

"But I didn't do it!" Pieter protested.

"Close those lips!" Monsieur Snippy scolded. "Oh, look, see? You've smudged it. I'll have to reapply the gloss."

Pieter tried to ignore the dreadful transformation of his face. He tried to think only of a way to solve the Czar's murder, but it was almost impossible. Whenever he closed his eyes, he could only see his horrible, ghastly, gaudy face.

At last Monsieur Snippy moved away from the chair.

"*Voilà*," he said solemnly. "What do you think?"

Pieter stared at himself. He looked like a Fabergé egg. Painted by a five-year-old child. With a glitter obsession.

"It's lovely," said Pieter weakly. "Please will you execute me now?"

"Do not be so impatient!" said Monsieur Snippy. "There is still your hair! The face is the picture, but a picture is nothing without a good frame."

From another drawer, the executioner brought out a wig, square like a hedgerow, only cotton-candy pink. He put it on Pieter's head. Then he fetched his diamond pruning shears and started to snip. Locks and curls fell steadily onto the floor of the chamber as Monsieur Snippy worked. A hairstyle began to emerge: the shape of a palm tree, with a long leaning trunk of hair, and dangly fronds sprouting from the top. Monsieur Snippy tied the fronds into a dozen plaited pigtails, then with rainbow ribbons he hung bells and baubles and candy canes.

"When your head flies off into the crowd," he explained, "these little presents scatter into the audience." He clapped his hands together. "I *love* Yuletide!"

Then he dressed Pieter in a huge frilly yellow dress, with stilettos so tall they were more like stilts.

"Look at you!" he said.

Pieter looked. In the mirror, a pantomime dame who

was the victim of an explosion at a makeup shop looked back at him.

"Now for the main event!" said Monsieur Snippy, clapping his hands together. "Chop, chop, Pieter! The crowds are waiting!"

Ugor and Lord Xin barged into the tallychamber, took one look at Pieter, and immediately burst into hysterics. They pointed at his dress, his wig, his face with all its ridiculous makeup . . . Pieter closed his eyes and tried to shut the laughter out, but it was impossible.

Now he understood the terrifying truth about Monsieur Snippy. It wasn't just a simple case of subtracting the head from the shoulders. Before Pieter was executed, he would be made to die from shame.

I give up! thought Pieter's brain. *Kill me now! I can't stand it!*

"Keep thinking about the murder!" he told it. "Find the culprit!"

"What are you saying, Tallymaster? Rehearsing last words?" Lord Xin dabbed a tear from his eye.

"You know that I'm innocent!" Pieter said, tottering forward on his high heels.

The Heirmaster shrugged. "Perhaps," he said. "Perhaps not. You're still a traitor. If you hadn't been a hostage, I would have chopped your head off months ago."

"Alexander will save me," Pieter answered.

"Alexander *not even recognize you*," Ugor said, grinning. "That why we hired Monsieur Snippy."

Panic took hold of Pieter. He knew then that he was doomed. His brain had failed him, Alexander would ignore him . . . Only Teresa could save him now.

He tried to struggle, but Ugor and Lord Xin held him firmly by the elbows and marched him down the stairs. The maids, bringing back struggling nets of poor blackbirds to bake in a pie for Alexander's Yuletide supper, all turned to laugh at him. Ugor barged them aside, and carried Pieter through the Hall of Faces, where Alexander sat curled up at the far end.

"Alexander!" he yelled. "It's me, P—"

Ugor's scarred and smelly hand clamped over his mouth. Alexander did not even look up as Pieter was carried across the hall (even the eyes of the portraits seemed to sparkle with mirth) and shoved out into the courtyard.

"Behold!" Lord Xin cried. "The traitorous Tallymaster, the murderer of our beloved czar: Pieter Abadabacus!"

Sunlight blinded him, but Pieter heard the huge sucking sound of a thousand people all gasping at once. Squinting through the glare, he found himself standing on an execution platform built from timber. The enormous crowd of Petrossia folk stood before him. Row upon row of heads, like an endless field of winter turnips. Pieter had never seen so many people all with the same frozen expression of shock.

Then there was a deafening roar as they all split their sides laughing.

"HA-HA-HA-HA-HA!"

To Pieter, each hoot, tee-hee, and titter hurt worse than anything he had ever known. Monsieur Snippy, without laying a finger on Pieter, was torturing him in the most excruciating way. His insides were twisting and squirming, while his whole body burned with shame. And all the while, the crowd laughed and laughed and laughed. Hot tears streamed down their faces and froze solid on their cheeks. This was better than a Yuletide play.

Pieter fell to his knees, unable to take any more. Monsieur Snippy gave a cold smile and clicked his fingers. At once Ugor came forward and hoisted Pieter up.

"I had hoped to make you die of shame," said Monsieur Snippy in his ear. "Alas, I will have to execute you in the normal way." The executioner took a step backwards and fetched his diamond shears.

"Any last words?" Lord Xin asked.

The noise of the crowd ebbed to snickers and chuckles, as everyone waited to see what Pieter might say.

One of the amazing things about geniuses is that their brains never stop working. Even then, moments from death, Pieter was still searching for an answer to the Czar's murder, trying out different combinations of the facts. He had arranged them in a million different ways, but somehow they would just not fit into a solution.

The broken glass.

The sleeping kitten.

The locked room.

The cloud of specks.

Now he was out of time. Ugor and Lord Xin stepped backwards. Monsieur Snippy donned a raincoat and a little umbrella hat to stop the blood from staining his outfit. He clacked his diamond shears together and advanced. . . .

And then suddenly: *click*. The various clues slotted into place like cogs in a machine, and Pieter whirred to life.

"WAIT!" he screamed. "I'VE GOT IT! I'VE GOT THE ANSWER!"

The crowd burst out laughing again, but this time Pieter didn't care.

He had the solution!

He had the answer!

He knew who had murdered the Czar!

Unfortunately, at that moment Monsieur Snippy's diamond shears clipped together. Pieter felt a sharp pinching sensation in his neck—and his head flew off his shoulders in a fountain of blood.[22]

Up into the air it went, the head spinning, all the gifts and baubles on his ridiculous wig flying off and scattering into the crowd of Petrossia folk, who all yelled things like:

"Wow!"

And, "A candy cane!"

And, "This is the best Yuletide ever!"

Pieter's head thumped on the wooden platform. His body keeled over. No one was laughing now. A few old babushkas, who felt sorry for the poor boy genius, whispered prayers for his soul. Amna, still feverishly writing letters up in the aviary, let out a scream and began to wail.

Mostly, though, the crowd was silent. They stood there, aching a little. Perhaps it was from the laughter. Perhaps the cold. Perhaps the sadness.

Monsieur Snippy stepped forward, wiped his blood-splattered shears on a hanky, and tossed it to the crowd.

"*Voilà*," he said. "Happy Yuletide. Pieter is dead."

---

22. Ugor, standing too close, was thoroughly splattered. Ever since that Yuletide, Father Frost outfits have tended to be red, rather than blue.

(A NOTE ON GRUESOMENESS)

Because this story is a true fairy tale, it gets rather *grim* at times. There's already been a murder. Now our hero's head has been sliced off. And later on, things will get even more grisly.

But don't worry. Pieter hasn't actually died—because this is a fairy tale.

And there is a happy ending of sorts—because it is also true.

3

Pieter Minus His Head

After Monsieur Snippy's announcement, there was a moment of stillness, followed by a blood-curdling shriek.

Lord Xin had drawn his knife. Shaking, he pointed it down at Pieter's severed head. The rest of the crowd gasped as they saw why.

The head had *opened its eyes*. And then suddenly, it *spoke*.

"Ooh," Pieter said woozily. "What happened? Where was I? Oh yes!" He grinned. "Listen, everyone! I've solved it! I know who murdered the Czar!"

CLUNK. Monsieur Snippy fainted and fell off the platform. Nobody noticed. Everyone was staring in utter horror as the undead head of Pieter Abadabacus talked on and on, without stopping.

"It's simple really. On that day when Alexander first became a kitten, he brought something with him down from the kitchen shelf. Or rather," said Pieter, feeling the words build up in him, like steam, "or rather, he brought lots of little things with him. Little, black, jumping, blood-sucking things. Understand?"

The crowd in the courtyard said nothing. They were frozen to the spot with terror.

"Of course you understand!" Pieter went on. "You all know what I'm talking about! And when Alexander drank the Gargantua, it went into his blood, and when they drank his blood, it went into them too . . . It didn't just make *him* bigger and bigger, it increased the size of his *fleas*!"

Pieter grinned triumphantly. Everything suddenly fell into place. It hadn't even been a murder at all! The giant fleas had only done what came naturally to them: bitten skin in search of blood. Alexander, who had swimming pools of the stuff, could manage without a few gallons (even if the fleas did keep him rather thin and hungry—no wonder he was always ravenous). The Czar, however, was doomed.

Pieter's shout had startled them into jumping away, out through the stained-glass door, breaking the glass. And the Slinjas had never seen anyone because the murderers had been miniscule that day when Alexander had lapped up his first saucer of milk. It was only through the winter, as they sipped again and again on Alexander's alchemical blood, that they had grown steadily bigger: from full stops, to small spots, to large black blobs.

"The greatest conqueror of all time," said Pieter in wonder. "Killed by fleas."[23]

Although, Pieter thought, this was only partly true. It was the Czar's ambition, after all, that had led to his death. It had been his obsession to change his son. *His* ambition. *His* greed. His insatiable desire to conquer had, in the end, conquered him.

"So you see?" Pieter said at last. "I *didn't* murder the Czar! If anything, he murdered himself! You can't execute me when I'm innocent! Where's Monsieur Snippy? Tell him to halt the execution at once! You can't kill me, I . . ." Pieter trailed off. "Wait a second. Why can't I feel my body?"

Noticing it lying several feet away from him, Pieter screamed.

So did Ugor.

So did everyone else.

---

23. No one knows what happened to the Czar's killers for certain, but many years later on the island of Avalon there lived a group of fleas who were, by all accounts, really enormous. This fleamily (like a family, only smaller and jumpier) lived in an old top hat, and it is extremely likely they were the descendants of the tiny assassins who escaped the Royal Palace that day. Born before their parents' alchemy-infused blood had worn off, this fleamily became the first of a brand-new species: the biggest and rarest fleas the world.

What's more, the fleamily could speak, and hopped about on two legs. Drinking a mix of Gargantua and Catastrophica potions, along with the Czar's blood, had also had a most surprising side effect: it had made the fleas more human too.

For more information, read the story of Hercuflor, visit the shop called Happy Ever Afters, and ask for Mr. Stickler.

4

Death Goes on Holiday

After the crowd stampeded in panic from the palace—

After Ugor revived Monsieur Snippy—

After the executioner fainted a second time—

After Pieter's body sat up, neck still spurting blood, and tried to wander off before falling from the stage—

After Lord Xin called a priest, who tried with no success to convince Pieter's soul to leave his body—

After Monsieur Snippy was taken away to the Gloom Room for performing an incompetent beheading—

After the courtyard was cordoned off until Pieter *finally* decided to hop off to Heaven or Hell or Limbo or Wherever—

After a whole day passed—

After his head and body were *still alive*—

After rumors about Pieter swept through the kingdom—

(I heard he's a zombie—)

(No, obviously a vampyr necromancer—)

(No, clearly an undead Lich King—)

After all this happened . . .

Yet *more* strange occurrences befell the land of Petrossia. At Yuletide supper in the Winter Palace, five hundred blackbirds all burst from the pie that Empurrer Alexander was about to gobble up, even though the chefs had cooked it in their ovens until the pastry was golden brown.

Empurrer Alexander didn't mind, though, and leaped about the Hall of Faces, swallowing up all the poor panicked creatures as they fluttered around the rafters. But afterward, he lay on the ground on his side, hissing and groaning, whilst inside his belly there could be heard the frightened chirruping of a whole flock of birds that were somehow still alive in his stomach even after being eaten.

The Royal Vet was called, but before he could get there, Alexander let out a strangled meow, and with a rasping farting sound, all five hundred blackbirds flew from his bottom in a huge black cloud, and vanished out the unmended stained-glass doors.

When Alexander finally got tenderly to his feet, he found he had accidentally been lying on the butler. The poor man was squashed flat as a pancake, yet when the others came to scrape him off the carpet, he opened his eyes and began to talk to them. Unable to be a butler anymore, he was folded up and posted in an envelope to the Slinjas, to see what they could make of him.

As Bloom began to thaw the frozen roads and warm the icy winds, reports began to reach the palace of yet more peculiar occurrences happening all over the country.

A drowned sailor from Port Xanderberg, whose ship had been sunk off the coast by the pirate Dreadbeard, suddenly walked out of the beach surf one morn, after stumbling blindly across the sea bed for three days.

A rich duchess paid a small fortune in gold to get one of the last eggs not yet gobbled by Alexander, yet when it was boiled and she broke the shell with her silver spoon, out hatched a fluffy yellow chick that ran across her dining table, crying *cheep-cheep-cheep*.

It wasn't just Pieter—not a man or beast in the whole kingdom could *die*. They just kept lingering on, when they ought to be passing away.

This was the final straw for the Czar's armies. Not only did they have a ruler who wasn't interested in conquering, but now they were in a country where no one could be killed: their favorite hobby was completely ruined.

The barbarians mutinied, and set up their own kingdom

of Barbaria to the west.[24] The Mongols made Lord Xin their Khan Prince, and went on the rampage to the east.

The Slinja bodyguards turned sideways and slipped away through cracks in the walls. Freed from his oath, Sir Klaus flew away on the back of a blackbird. Only Warmaster Ugor—most loyal of the War Council—remained at the Winter Palace.

By the time the first blossoms appeared, the Czar's mighty empire had gone with the wind and frost. All that was left of his once-vast kingdom was his Winter Palace, the River Ossia, and the dark hills and forests around it.

And Death *still* hadn't turned up anywhere.

Pieter thought back to the skeleton with the scythe, that had come to fetch the soul of Bloodbath. He wondered why Grim hadn't shown up for Pieter, or anyone else in Petrossia.

Maybe he was running late.

Perhaps he'd overslept.

Or taken a Yuletide holiday?

Pieter had his own theory. He didn't know how she'd done it, but it had to be her. Who else could it be? There was

---

24. In the Kingdom of Barbaria, everyone had to wear beards, even women and children. It was also a criminal offense to do unbarbaric things like read poetry, cuddle rabbits, and talk about your feelings (unless they were feelings of rage, hatred, or bloodlust).

only one person he knew who could work actual miracles.

Somehow, Teresa Gust had saved his life. Pieter was sure of it.

There was only one problem with his theory: if it was true, then why was she still missing?

(A NOTE ON DEATH)

There are some readers right now who might be saying to themselves things like:

"A country where nobody can die? That sounds a lot like heaven!"

And, "I wouldn't mind living in Petrossia!"

Or, "So it's just like a fairy tale, and everyone gets to live happily ever after?"

These readers are wrong. A country without death would be an utterly dreadful place. Just think about it.

First of all, there's the problem of *room*. With no one dying but babies still being born, Petrossia is gradually filling up with people. More and more and more of them. Eventually, it will grow so crowded that everyone will have to stand on one another's heads.

Then, there's the fact that eternal *life* does not equal eternal *youth* (just as Grimaldi the Most Wise proved). People are still growing older. And balder. And wrinklier. And so on. *Forever.*

Eventually, people will grow so ancient that their brains will shrink to the size of Brussels sprouts and then evaporate out their ears. The only topic of conversation will be "The Good Old Days." Walking-stick manufacturers won't ever go out of business, but that is about the only plus.

Yes, a land of eternal life is a terrible place indeed. Life without death just feels wrong, like a sentence that won't end, but just keeps building and building, trying to reach a moment that never comes, until it starts to run out of things to say, and just repeats itself, saying the same old thing, again and again, repeating itself, and so on, and so forth, et cetera, et cetera, et cetera. . . .

You see? Life needs death the way a sentence needs a full stop.

Petrossia had a big problem. It needed fixing, fast.

5

Priest to Meet You

The Petrossia folk could deal with bitter winters and cruel rulers and next to no food, but now they had had enough. People began to pack their things and leave. The cooks, the maids, the guards . . . one by one they all went south like the geese, until the corridors of the Winter Palace were empty and silent, and only the defrosting heads on spikes stood watch at the gates.

"We ought to leave too," Amnabushka said to Pieter's head the next morn, when she shuffled up the stairs with his cup of khave (and a bucket to catch it in once he'd drunk it). "Find a trundle wagon and ride it west until we're a million miles old."

Despite everything, Amna made Pieter smile. It was hard to believe there'd been a time when he'd been rude about her magic. In a way, she was mightier than he'd ever realized.

"A fairy folkmother and a talking head!" she said. "We'll make a fair living telling fortunes. Especially at a time like this. We'll save up until we can pay a doctor to stitch your body back on. One of the maids told me about a surgeon from Ingolstadt who—"

Pieter shook his head. Or tried to. "I can't leave, Amna." He didn't need to tell her why. Across the rest of the continent, life was still starting and ending like it always had. It was only in Petrossia that nothing could die. If Pieter crossed the western border into Hertz, his life might leave his head in a heartbeat (or a lack of one).

"You should go," he told her, trying not to think any more about death and dying. "There's nothing keeping you here."

Amna looked quite cross at the suggestion. "There's a wildfolk saying: *There aren't many miles in a one-wheeled wagon.*" She leaned down and kissed his stone-cold cheek. "Which means, we go together or not at all."

Pieter tried to swallow the lump that was stuck in his throat, but it rose like a bubble into his head, pushing the hot tears out of his blurry eyes.

"Thank you, Amna," he managed to whisper. "Thank you."

The old Baba Sister touched the abacus bead, a new charm she had tied into her hair, and looked pleased. "He thanks me twice now! How could I abandon a boy with such manners?"

Somewhere in the Winter Palace, a grandpapa clock chimed two of the morn. The hallways belonged to the mice and the moonbeams. From down in the kitchens came the faint sound of a pig left oinking inside an oven, even though the last chef, before they left, had roasted it for hours and shoved an apple in its gob to shut it up. In the tallychamber, tinderflies crackled and snapped as they snoozed on their sugarstick stumps.

A hooded figure robed in black moved silently up the stairs.

It seemed to be carrying some sort of long stick with a pointy metal thing on the end.

The hooded figure opened the door to the tallychamber and glided inside.

A head lay snoring on a velvet pillow.

Soundlessly, the figure in black crept closer. Closer. There were only two possibilities: either the figure knew exactly where to step, or the old floorboards were too terrified to make a creak and draw attention to themselves.

"Ahem," said the figure.

The head snored on.

"Oi." The figure in black reached out and flicked the head on the nose. "You."

Pieter snorted, yawned, and sleepily opened his eyes. "Amna? What time is it?"

He looked up at the figure before him, taking in the blackness of the hood and the long sticklike thing it carried.

"Oh," he said. "It's *you*. I was beginning to think you weren't going to show up."

Pieter had been expecting this visit. After his near-death experience in the Gloom Room, he'd known it was only a matter of time before he came face-to-face again (or face-to-skull) with the skeleton called Grim. Strangely, he didn't feel afraid. Perhaps it was because he could no longer feel his heart race, or his spine shiver, or his kneecaps quake.

"You're late, you know," he said, trying to fill the awkward silence. "People have been concerned. Come on, then. Hurry up and take me to the land of the dead. There's quite a long line behind me, you know. You really haven't been doing your job very—"

The figure threw back its hood.

"Oh," said Pieter. "It's *you*. What do you want?"

Ugor seized him up by the hair. His eyes were red and crazed. Pieter could smell barbeeri on his breath.[25]

"What Ugor wants?" he said, shaking Pieter in his huge fist. "Czar alive! Empire back! No more beetroot soup for dinner! And most of all Ugor wants Tallymaster DEAD!"

One of the advantages of his current predicament was

25. Barbeeri: a gloopy mix of beer, pig's blood, iron fillings, and beard sweat, that no one with more than a twenty-word vocabulary can stomach.

that Pieter didn't feel scared by death threats anymore. Ugor could rant and rave at him as much as he wanted, but what could he possibly do? Chop Pieter's head off again?

"Wait a minute." Pieter noticed for the first time that the long stick Ugor had set aside was not actually a scythe. "Why have you brought a shovel?"

Ugor chuckled. His laugh was a scarred and ugly thing, just like him.

"Tallymaster won't die," he said, "but Ugor can still *bury* you."

Pieter had always imagined that death would be the scariest thing that could happen to him. But now that he *was* dead, he realized there were worse things.

Like being buried in a coffin . . .

Like having to lie underground for centuries, while the worms wriggled and the roots wrapped round him like fingers. . . .

Like being trapped in total darkness, forever . . .

"Exactly," said Ugor when Pieter explained all that to him.

"Amna!" Pieter yelled. "Amnabushka Baba Gale, help!"

Ugor seized up a ball of paper from the tallychamber's overflowing bin and stuffed it in Pieter's mouth. "Priest? Come up here! Bring coffin!"

In the doorway, the priest appeared. He was very short.

He wore crisp white robes, clean and billowy as bedsheets, and a name badge that said "Holy Father Robin—*Priest to meet ya!*" His face was mostly a beard that looked like black sheep's wool. He carried a small, box-shaped coffin.

"Oh, Saint Ivan protect us!" Father Robin said in his high-pitched voice when his eyes fell upon Pieter. "When the dead refuse to die, the End of the World is surely nigh! Warmaster Ugor, *must* I bury this thing? My graveyard is very quiet. I do not want an undead head coming in and causing a ruckus. It might encourage the other corpses."

Ugor took his blundergun from his shoulder and aimed it at Father Robin. The barrel was like the end of a trombone. "You bury him," he said. "Or I bury *you*."

Father Robin's fluffy beard trembled. He opened his mouth to protest, but the only thing that came out was a sort of strangled warble, similar to the sound he might make during hymns. He clutched at his big wooden rosary beads. They were the size of hazelnuts.

In fact, Pieter realized, they *were* hazelnuts.

And as he realized this, Father Robin jammed them into the barrel of the blundergun.

Ugor was momentarily stunned. So was Pieter. It wasn't until they saw the priest yank off his fake beard with one hand, and reach up with a blazing pip chili in the other, that either of them realized what was happening, and who Father Robin really was.

By then, Teresa had already stuffed the red-hot chili into Ugor's bellybutton.

"YOWWW!" Ugor howled, or maybe it was, "YOUUU!"

The Warmaster yanked at the blazing pip, then roared as the green stalk broke off in his clumsy fists, leaving the red chili still lodged in his hairy gut. He swiped at Teresa like a wounded bear. She ducked under his legs as his fists sent volumes of books tumbling off the shelves, then he smashed the bed in two with a headbutt. Pieter tumbled headfirst onto the rug and Teresa booted him like a soccer ball, then dived after him like she was trying to save her own shot. The world whirled around them as they both rolled under the desk.

"Say your prayers!" Ugor bellowed above them.

And then, because he was sizzling so much with rage and pain that it had made him stupid, the Warmaster pulled the trigger on his blundergun.

There was a kind of stifled-farting sound from the trombone end, as the enormous explosive power of the gunpowder ignited, traveled down the barrel in search of something to blow up, and found the hazelnut.

Beneath the desk, Pieter shut his eyes as Teresa threw her hands around him. There was a bright flash like thunder that he saw behind his lids, a second of searing heat, a shriek of tearing metal, and finally just the smell of toasted hazelnut.

When Pieter looked out from under the desk, Ugor had been blown backwards into the wall, his face blackened and scorched. The blundergun was still in his hands. It had blossomed out in all directions, like the petals of a brass flower. The barbarian's mouth was open, his eyes were dazed, and the tip of his beard was smoking like an incense stick.

Pieter spat out the ball of paper. He found himself babbling. "Teresa? How can . . . What was . . . Is this a . . ." He took a deep breath and finally managed to ask an actual question. "Where have you *been*?"

"Brewing potions," she said. "Watch."

As a dazed Ugor tried to get up and out of the wall, Teresa rolled back out from under the wreckage of the desk. Her hands disappeared beneath her priest robes, and came out again with something silver and glinting.

A glass bottle, shaped like a *J*.

Twisting off the cork, she poured the alchemical gloop down over Ugor. The top of his head began to fizz. The Warmaster's huge belly first wobbled and then collapsed like a burnt soufflé. Tiny glittering discs began to drop from his body and clatter onto the floorboards. One of them rolled over to Pieter.

It was a coin. A gold rouble. The back of it had Ugor's face stamped on it, instead of the Czar's.

Teresa had just turned the Warmaster into a pile of money.

"Mammonia," she said, tossing the empty alchemical bottle into the bin. "It's weak alchemy. A few months at most, and it'll wear off." She turned to look back at Pieter. "Hey," she said quietly.

Pieter looked up at his best and long-lost friend, and wondered what to say back. It felt like a lifetime ago since they had last said goodbye to each other. Actually, for Pieter, it really was. What words could possibly sum up everything that had happened since then?

He eventually settled just on stating the obvious.

"Hey," he said back. "Your disguise is on fire."

Teresa looked behind her and yelped, swatting out the smoke sizzling from her Father Robin robes. Finally she gave up, and just pulled off the whole disguise—the white vestment, the wig, the rubber wrinkles—until it all lay in a heap on the floor.

Teresa had changed. She wore her same suit of patchwork pockets and colored ropes, but hanging from her grappling hooks now were clinking, swinging bottles. Dozens of alchemical potions. Some were long, thin, and green as runner beans; others were tiny and round and red as cherries; still more were yellow and curved as bananas. She was taller than he remembered, or perhaps he was just a lot shorter. Her hair had grown back a little, and she had plaited it again, but the starlight and moon-white colorings had washed away from her, leaving her green-eyed and dark.

"I missed you," she said.

"I missed you too."

She looked down at his neck, and smiled weakly. "You're missing lots of things."

Pieter shrugged, then remembered he didn't have shoulders. "Maybe," he said. "But at least I've found my friend."

6

Escapes, Reunions, and Revelations

After rushing down the North Spire and waking Amna—

After hugging and laughing and calling for Alexander—

After yelling his name, and running toward the Hall of Faces, and throwing open the doors, and kissing his nose, and high-fiving his paws—

After Alexander's tears had soaked all the floors, and after he purred to show how he'd missed her—

After telling him Teresa was really his sister—

And he was her brother—

And they were a family and finally together—

And nothing could part them, not now and not ever—

Teresa told them about her escape from Petrossia.

The three of them lay on Alexander's upturned paw as if it was a sofa, while his enormous face beamed down like an orange sun. Pieter had not seen the Empurrer this happy since before his sixth birthday. Amna was laughing and tying the *Priest to meet ya!* badge into her hair as a new charm, while Teresa told the tale of her escape from Petrossia.

It turns out the rumors had all been true—more or less. After escaping up the chimney while Pieter and Amna had become the Czar's hostages, Teresa hid up on the rooftop for days, surviving on pigeon eggs and frozen gutter water. She spent the days huddled over the chimney pots with blue shaking hands, trying to keep warm, while the wind ran through her like a wolf runs through a forest, swift and howling and hungry for her heat.

At night, she crept down to the Winter Palace, trying to stir up trouble.

MIRROR, MIRROR ON THE WALL,
WHO'S THE WORST KING
OF THEM ALL?

. . . she wrote in dust on one of the hallway mirrors.

Next, she arranged the leaves of the runner bean plants in the Winter Palace glasshouse so they spelled out: *PEAS, NOT WAR.*

The Czar was furious. He ordered the hallway mirror smashed and crushed—and the peas mashed and mushed.

"Let that be a lesson to anyone or any*thing* that dares to defy me," he announced.

But the next day, a bunch of kindling told the Czar *YOU'RE FIRED* (the Czar ordered it to be burned to death), and a disused toilet in the South Wing was discovered saying: *IF THE CZAR THINKS HE CAN SCARE ME, HE'S POTTY.*

It seemed like the Winter Palace itself was rising up against the tyrannical king. But the Czar knew better.

"It's the Spice Monkey!" he growled. "She's still here somewhere, using the chimneys to sneak about! Trying to distract us so she can rescue her friends."

From that moment on, every hearth was kept roaring hot, every flue was filled with choking smoke, and Teresa could no longer climb up and down her secret corridors to stir up trouble. There was nothing she could do but run.

After she fled the Winter Palace, Sir Klaus chased Teresa halfway across the Empire. There are stories as long as this one that tell of the deadly games of hide-and-seek Teresa and the Spymaster had played across the rooftops of Muscov, through the forests of Tumber, and beneath the sewers of Günkel. Twice the Spymaster had caught her, and twice she had escaped him again before he could return her to the Czar.

Finally, cornered in Port Xanderberg, Teresa hid inside a barrel of pickled catfish, where she nibbled on fish tails and sipped vinegar-water for three days, until a ship rolled her onboard and set sail across the Boreal Sea, to Albion.

"But I took someone with me," she told them as they sat there, all together again.

"Who did you take?" Amna asked. "Tell us."

Teresa said, "I took Blüstav."

Pieter frowned as he remembered the name. "The Czar's old Alchemaster? I thought he was a pile of coins, like Ugor."

"You're right, he was. But Blüstav is useless at alchemy. His potions leak away and quickly wear off. He had changed back from the pile of coins months ago. I met him in an underground dungeon in Port Xanderberg—this was way back in Worsen, the second time Sir Klaus caught me. Blüstav was chained up for stealing alchemy books. Boasted he'd thieved whole libraries full of books—starting with those from the Duke of Madri's treasure chamber when he first turned back into a man. Claimed he'd *borrowed* those. Ha! But he'd been caught by the Czar's men in Xanderberg. He's a crafty old man, and a liar and a crook, but he gave me an idea. I freed us both, and promised to become his apprentice."

Amna frowned. "I thought he was a fraud," she said.

"I *know* he's a fraud," said Teresa. "But he's useful too. I needed a place to hide, and a way to practice alchemy, and Blüstav has his own laboratory in Albion. He's got more alchemicals than I can mix together, and more recipe books than I could ever read. I've been studying them from dawn to dusk." She jabbed her thumbs at all the alchemicals tinkling from her grappling hooks. "Look at all the alchemy I can do now!"

Pieter gazed at the bottles, feeling a little jealous. Bloom and Swoon and many a moon ago, alchemy had been something he and Teresa had done together. Did she no longer need him anymore?

"I'm surprised he didn't sell you back to the Czar as soon as he found out who you were," said Amna.

"He would've," said Teresa craftily, "if I wasn't so good at lying. I never told Blüstav about the *real* aim of Operation: *His Royal Whiskers*. Made up some other story. *Besides*, my alchemy is making him rich. Blüstav sells it to rich customers and pretends it's his own."

"A very bad-mannered man," said Amna, shaking her head.

Teresa shrugged. "He even had the Czar request a flea-lotion for Alexander." She pointed at one of the nozzle-spray bottles swinging from her suit. "I told Blüstav I'd take it personally to the docks, then sailed back here on a rescue mission!" She smiled. "I gave him a potion of my own making so he'll sleep until I'm back."

Pieter looked down at his lack of a body. "You're a bit late anyway."

Teresa slumped her shoulders, crestfallen. "I know. I was halfway to Port Xanderberg when I heard the Czar had been murdered. When I finally got back here, I found Amna with her charms taken, Alexander with his heart broken, and you—" Her voice cracked. She picked up the priest robes, dabbed her eyes, and blew her nose. "Oh, Pieter, I'm so sorry."

Pieter didn't feel sad, only bewildered. "I really thought *you'd* done this somehow," he told her. "I thought you'd stopped death, just in Petrossia, using alchemy or magic or something. . . ."

"This didn't happen because of me," Teresa said darkly. "It's happened because of *him*."

"Who?" said Amna, but even as she asked, Pieter knew the answer.

"Holy Sohcahtoa," he gasped. "Not the Czar?"

Teresa nodded. "The Czar."

There was a low, loud hiss above them as Alexander bared his saber teeth.

"But it can't be." A shiver ran up Pieter's neck. "The Czar is *dead*."

"That's exactly why it *has* to be him," said Teresa. "Didn't he always boast he would do it? He's gone and conquered Death."

7

The Psycho and the Psychopomp

Was Teresa right? Had the Czar really conquered the land of the dead? Pieter wasn't sure. He liked to check and recheck an answer—particularly if it was a terrifying one.

"We can't know that for sure," he insisted." Only Alexander was there when the Czar died. And he was asleep!"

Teresa nodded back at him. "You're right. At first, I only had my suspicions. But I knew I was right. Death stops working, on the very day the Czar dies? It's too much of a coincidence! What are the odds?"

Pieter opened his mouth to tell her, but she pressed a finger to his lips.

"So," she continued. "Traveling back toward the Winter Palace, I started looking for proof. If the Czar really had conquered Death, then surely there'd be evidence? Maybe even a witness. I looked all over, but it was hopeless. The whole country is in a mess. Barbarians fighting in the west, Prince Xin rampaging in the east . . . It would have taken me a thousand years to find what I needed. Luckily, I had help."

"Help?" Pieter frowned. "Who from?"

Teresa grinned. "An expert."

Pursing her lips, she whistled a tune up at the rafters. One of the blackbirds roosting there sang the same melody back at her, and dived down toward them.

In its claws, it held a little leather pouch. On its beak, it wore a tiny string bridle and reins. And on its back, it carried a small white rider.

Before Pieter could cry out, before Amna could swat the mouse with her broom, before Alexander even spotted him at all, Sir Klaus the Spymaster swooped down on his blackbird steed and landed on Teresa's shoulder.

But instead of drawing his venomous sword, he doffed his hat and bowed. "Your Majesty," he said into her ear. "I am your humble servant."

Pieter looked at Teresa, dumbfounded.

She just blushed, and shrugged.

"I caught Princess Teresa twice," explained Sir Klaus in his quiet and solemn voice. "But the third time we met, she captured *me*."

"With cheese?" asked Pieter.

"With the *truth*," Sir Klaus said severely. "Once I discovered that Princess Teresa was rightful heir to the Iron Crown, I took a solemn oath to serve her the moment she returned to Petrossia. She commanded me to learn how the Czar had conquered Death."

"And you *did* find out," said Teresa, pulling on her gloves. "Without you, we wouldn't know the truth."

Sir Klaus's nose flushed pink, and he bowed. "My Patra. I only hope that I can make amends for some of the wrong I did in the service of the Czar. There was no honor in following that tyrant. I was a fool."

"Just remember what I told you," said Teresa, taking the little leather pouch from the claws of the blackbird on her shoulder. "Your oath is to serve the Petrossia folk, not any king or queen."

Sir Klaus tipped his budgie-feathered hat, and hopped back onto his blackbird. "Then I fly north," he said. "To the Waste. And from this day, I swear to do all I can to keep the people of Petrossia safe. Maybe in that way, I can redeem myself. Fare thee well."

"Fare thee well," said Teresa to the solemn little creature, as one gloved hand began to loosen the drawstring pouch he had brought to her.

"Careful, my Patra," Sir Klaus warned, hand on the pommel of his sword. "It is accursed. Everything it touches drops down dead. I had to chop it into pieces."

Then he spurred his blackbird into flight, flitted away through the open doorway, and was gone.[26]

---

26. Sir Klaus kept his oath. He flew out of this story and into many others, and always upheld his promise to keep the people of Petrossia safe. Forming a band of Mousketeers around him, he guarded the last vial of Black Death plague, sealed deep inside the Czar's northern fortress. He did so for such a long time, it was even rumored that the Pale Traveler, who leads souls to the land of the dead, kept conveniently "forgetting" to collect Sir Klaus, on account of the work the mouse was saving him by keeping the Black Death from killing everyone.

Amna began to chuckle. "What an alchemist, my Patra is! She somehow changed the Spymaster!"

Pieter started to laugh too, but he soon stopped when Teresa cupped one gloved hand, and carefully upended Sir Klaus's leather bag. Out into her covered palm, she poured twenty-seven bones (Pieter counted exactly), no bigger than pebbles.

If he had still had a heartbeat, it would have been racing. Beside him, Amna gasped softly. Alexander's growl rumbled around the room. Instantly, Sir Klaus was forgotten.

Because the little white bones were twitching in Teresa's gloves. They were *alive.*

"Evidence," Teresa said, as one by one she popped the bones back in place. "Proof that this is the work of the Czar. Sir Klaus said he found it on the rooftop, scuttling around the gutters. Who knows how it managed to get up there?"

Teresa clicked the last bone back in place, then plucked the skeleton's hand up by the wrist and held it out for them to see. It wriggled in her grip like a five-legged tarantula.

"The Pale Traveler," Amna quailed, touching her hair for a charm that was no longer there.

Pieter stared at the skeletal hand.

"When Sir Klaus first brought it to me," said Teresa, "I tied a stick of charcoal to its fingers, and set it down on some paper." With her free hand, she took a wad of pages from a pocket, and held them up for everyone to see. "And look what it scribbled down."

Pieter and Amna stared at the hand's writing. It was messy, and jumbled, and written in a long spidery scrawl that went upside down and diagonally and all over.

But if you looked carefully, you could just make out the story.

The story started in the Hall of Faces on Yuletide morn, when the Czar woke to find a skeleton looming over him. It leaned down and offered a bony hand at the exact moment he opened his eyes. In its eye sockets, two pupils glowed a warm and friendly yellow.

Hello! it said, grin wide. **Please vacate your body!**

The Czar never obeyed orders, especially not polite ones. He leaped up to fight the skeleton—then found he had done exactly as he had been asked. His soul billowed darkly in the air like a thundercloud, while his body lay at his feet in Alexander's fur.

"You must be Death," said the Czar, quickly recovering from his initial shock. He looked down at his corpse, then up at the skeleton's black cloak and scythe. "I've been looking forward to meeting you."

Oh, I'm not Death, corrected the skeleton. **I just work for him. I'm a psychopomp—it's my job to guide you to the land of the dead. Name's Grimaldi the Most Wise. But most people call me Grim.**

He held his hand out for the Czar to shake. The Czar gripped it and squeezed. Hard, until something went *pop*.

That's quite a handshake, said the skeleton, cracking his knucklebones back into place.

"And that," said the Czar, pointing above Grim, "is quite a scythe."

It was milky white and curved, like the end of one of Alexander's claws. Leaning closer, the Czar could actually *hear* the wicked invisible edge. A faint tinny roar, like putting your ear to a seashell. It was the sound, Grim explained, of phatoms screaming as they drifted onto the blade, were sliced in half, and fizzed away into nothingness.[27]

The Czar smiled when he heard that.

Not in a nice way.

"Sounds sharp," he said.

Grim nodded. **Sharp enough to cut through Time and Space. Every psychopomp in the world is given a soul-blade like this. Makes my job a lot easier. I mainly use it for shortcuts. Just two slashes and a slice, and I can make**

---

27. Phatoms are phantom molecules that the majority of the spirit worlds are made of. Not to be confused with fatoms, which make up the majority of cakes.

a doorway that will lead anywhere. The skeleton patted the scythe proudly. **The handle also has a compass attached.**

The Czar raised his eyebrows. "Ever tried cutting bone with it?" he asked innocently.

The skeleton's spine clicked as it straightened. **Wow,** he said. **That's a bit of a creepy question.**

"Sorry," said the Czar at once, grinning sheepishly.

I mean, you know you've crossed the line when the *living skeleton* is scared.

"I apologize," said the Czar, holding up his hands. "I'm not myself. I just wasn't expecting this. I had so much still to do."

If you have any unfinished business back in the land of the living, Grim said stiffly, **you're welcome to put in a request for a haunting. Otherwise, we should probably head off.**

"Yes," said the Czar, stroking his mustache and thinking. "Head off. My thoughts exactly."

This way then, said Grim. **It's a long journey.**

"Why don't we take that shortcut?" asked the Czar, pointing behind the skeleton.

Grim fell for it.

What shortcut? he said, turning.

With a well-aimed karate kick, the Czar sent Grim's skull soaring off his bony shoulders.

I *KNEW* THERE WAS SOMETHING CREEPY ABOUT YOU! Grim's head roared as it plonked down at his feet.

The Czar's grin of triumph was almost cut short. Very short indeed. Headless, Grim swung his scythe blindly, slicing off the glowing blue tip of the Czar's mustache. It flew off his cheek like a firework and dissolved into a thousand tiny sparking phatoms. That was a sharp blade: so keen it could cut your soul. It only made the Czar want it all the more.

Now he was careful, and took his time—with a series of vicious punches, he dislocated every joint in Grim's body. *Pop! Pop! Click!*

Ouch!

Gerroff!

That tickles!

Grim's arm bones fell from his rib cage, his legs fell from his hips, and just like that the skeleton collapsed into a heap of bones that rattled together like a creepy xylophone.

This is a clear violation of rule #129 of the Mortal Code!

The Czar tilted his head at Grim's mention of rules, and the suggestion that he ought to obey them.

Put me back together! I've got other souls to collect! Grim's eyes flared a panicked pink. **Hey, don't touch that!**

There was a snapping sound as the Czar broke off the

top of the scythe, and carefully twisted the bolted-on soul-blade upright, until he held it like a sword.

Do you have any idea what you've just done? Grim cried. **Vandal! Hooligan!**

"That," said the Czar, picking up the skull, "is no way to speak to your new king."

Grim, staring up at the Czar's mad gaze, did what almost everyone who fights the Czar does eventually.

He ran away.

In a dozen different directions.

Off went his bones, scattering left and right: feet hopping, knees hobbling, spine wriggling like a great ghoulish caterpillar. The Czar tied up the furry corners of Grim's cloak into a sack, then went hunting through Alexander's fur until he'd gathered the skeleton back up.

Only one hand managed to escape. It scuttled across the hall, fingertips clacking on the flagstones, and climbed up the chimney out of sight.

"Where were *you* going?" the Czar asked the skull. "I'm waiting."

Grim's jaw was clacking with fear. His pupils were shaking in their empty sockets.

Waiting? What for?

"For you to do your job," said the Czar, his smile glinting

like the soul-blade. "Show me the way to the land of the dead."

Now at last, Pieter understood why Grim hadn't arrived to collect his soul—why Grim hadn't arrived to collect anybody's soul—the Czar had broken him up like a jigsaw, and stolen all but twenty-seven of his pieces.

"The Czar is the problem," Teresa said with utter certainty, putting Grim's story down before Pieter could read any more. "What's the *solution*, though?"

Amna spoke up. "Rescue the Pale Traveler from the Czar," she said. "Give Petrossia back its guide between life and death."

"Ignoring the fact that we've tried and failed twice now to defeat the Czar . . ." Teresa said. "How do we mount a rescue mission to bring back a living skeleton from the land of the dead?"

Pieter sighed. "That's the impossible part," he said.

"But only a *little bit* impossible," Amna said.

"*Totally* impossible," said Pieter, adamant. "We need a guide to lead us to the land of the dead. That's the whole reason I'm stuck here."

"You don't need a guide," Amna said, looking at Grim's skeletal finger twitching. "All you need is a hand to lead the way."

PART FIVE
Ever After

"Mr. Emperor, your sword won't help you,
Sceptre and crown have no power here."

—DEATH, IN HEIDELBERG'S *TÖTENTANZ*

"It is very true," said the Poodle, with
austere dignity, "that I am small; but, sir,
I beg to observe that I am all dog."

—*FANTASTIC FABLES*, AMBROSE BIERCE

We only part to meet again.

—*BLACK-EYED SUSAN*, JOHN GAY

1

Crossing the Gray Sea

The fire burned hot beneath the starry sky. It threw up orange embers and long yellow flames from its fierce red heart. Shadows on the courtyard floor danced to its crackle and throb. Smoke curled up into the night, smudging the moon from Pieter's sight, and Amna's voice was clear and bright as she sang her spell of safe return.

"Bind you to the fire, it will," she told them as she drew the last hieroglyphs in the air. Teresa lay down in Alexander's paw with Pieter in her lap. "We'll keep it burning as long as you are gone. No matter where you are, you'll always see its glimmer in your eye. Just follow it if ever your soul is lost. It'll lead you back to us."

Pieter closed his eyes. The spell really did work: the fire's image was a bright beacon burning behind his lids. He hoped he'd still see it in the land of the dead. How else would they find their way back to their bodies?

"Take good care of us while we're gone!" Teresa hugged Amna fiercely. She would stay here while their souls went wandering, and make sure Teresa's body was warm and well fed, and that Pieter's head didn't start to go moldy.

"One word of advice," Teresa added. "Don't feed me cabbage. It's you who'll suffer."

"And one last advice for *you*," Amna said. "A great journey lies between you and the Czar. Miles beyond even a Tallymaster's counting. By the time you return, you'll both be older than Babapatra. I have told you all we wildfolk know of the way to death. Still, my old heart shudders when I think of the dangers you might face. But I know you will pass them if you do so together."

"We will," Pieter said. "After all, *There aren't many miles in a one-wheeled wagon*."

Amna beamed, and looked up at Alexander. "Do not worry for your sister. With this boy, she will be just fine."

Alexander looked away, tail flicking moodily. His ears had been stuffed with pillows from the palace bedrooms to block out Amna's song: he was not going to the afterlife with them. All his scowling and clawing up of courtyard cobbles had not changed Teresa's mind. She had just folded her arms and given him one of her looks (the one that only a big sister can give her little brother).

"You might have the body of a gigantic kitten now, but inside you've still got the soul of a six-year-old. You're staying behind to guard us, Alexander, and that's that. Don't look at me that way. Of course I'm allowed to give you orders. I'm your big sister: technically, I'm first in line for the throne. And I can actually sit in it too."

At last, Alexander bowed his head and blinked his eyes at them both. Teresa reached out and kissed his pink nose, then held Pieter up as Alexander's tongue, red and rough as a brick wall, scraped over his face.

"This is a whole new definition of the word soul mates," she murmured, taking off her gloves. Grim's hand was inside a box beside Pieter. All Teresa had to do was lift the lid and touch the skeletal fingers, and they would be pulled toward the land of the dead.

She hesitated. "What are the chances we'll come back?"

He calculated quickly. "Roughly one in five thousand, four hundred—"

"Stupid question, forget I asked," Teresa interrupted, and opened the box and tipped it onto her lap. Grim's hand tumbled out and tugged Pieter on the nose.

He felt something similar to a sneeze. Around him, the world washed away like a painting in the rain.

So it was that Pieter and Teresa took Grim's hand, and let it pull them into the world of the dead. Apart from the far-away glimmer of Amna's fire, their souls were the only shining lights in that gray and gloomy place. Pieter was the blue of clear skies, and Teresa was the color of a spring thunderstorm.

"Thank the afterlife!" she sighed, looking down at the ghostly outline of her Spice Monkey suit. "Our souls are wearing clothes. You won't believe how much time I spent worrying about that."

"I'm body shaped!" Pieter cried, feeling a sudden lurch of vertigo as he looked down from a much higher place than he was currently used to. *Legs, shoulders, knees, and toes*—all below his neck once more. And why wouldn't they be? Monsieur Snippy had executed his *body*, not his soul.

"This must be the place Amna told us about," Teresa said, turning her attention to the foggy world around them. "The Gray Sea, she called it, that separates the white of this life from the black of the next."

They stood under a sky the color of fog on a beach the color of ashes, watching as waves the color of slush broke across the shore. *Hush*, each one whispered as it slumped and dissolved. *Hush. Hush.*

Pieter shrugged. (Oh, it felt *good* to do that again.) "It certainly matches Amna's description."

Grim's hand crawled across the sand like a crab, heading toward an ancient rowboat that bobbed on a ragged rope in the surf.

"'And the Pale Traveler will lead you across,'" Teresa said, remembering one of the many wildfolk sayings Amna had shared with them before they went.

They followed the hand and got in, and the boat cast off by itself with no oars or rudder. Soon they had crested the waves and were gliding slowly out to sea.

There in the shallows, the rowboat passed over giant jellyfish creatures floating an arm's reach beneath the keel, like luminous orchids they could reach out and pluck. Their petaled fronds wilted and bloomed, wilted and bloomed as they drifted in the black water, and trapped in their long trailing tentacles were faint struggling souls, fuzzy and blue, no shape to them at all.

"Didn't Amna say something about the Lotus-Eaters?" Teresa said, grim-faced, as they both peered over the side. "The last living things that feed on the fringes of life. Those things have souls in their tentacles: they're eating memories. Look."

She pointed at the tentacles. Blue light from the souls was being sucked along them and into the center of each creature. Pieter saw faint pictures and shapes flickering there, like lanterns filled with dreams.

"Maybe they jumped in," Pieter said. "To forget."

"Or they were trying to swim back to their lives."

"Poor souls." He shuddered. "Why would they try and do that?"

"Same reason *we're* here, Pieter. Unfinished business."

The shore and the Lotus-Eaters disappeared as they sailed farther out. Soon there was nothing but gloomy dusk, and rippling water, and a horizon dividing the two. Amna's fire shrank down, smaller and fainter, until it was no more than a distant star, shining in the corners of their eyes.

A faint wind blew now and then in the stillness. Pieter couldn't stop shivering. Not because he was freezing—feeling the cold here was impossible. It was more that the memory of coldness made him shiver, just like his soul remembered that it was body shaped, and usually wore a Tallymaster outfit.

"Did you see how those souls beneath the water had gone all fuzzy?" he said. "Memories are powerful here. We're nothing without them."

Teresa lay back in the rowboat's seat and looked up at the sky. "Then we better not forget who we are."

But that was hard when their lives already seemed so far away, and it only got harder. Day never broke. Night never came. Time stood frozen. When Pieter and Teresa woke, haunted by the memory of hunger and thirst, the sky was still dusk and the water was still calm and the rowboat was still sailing ever onwards.

"Your hair's grown," he told Teresa one day when he woke. "Like Rapunzel's."

She stared back at him, expression blank and puzzled.

"You're wrong," she insisted, reaching up to touch her plait. "It's always been this long, since before we met."

Pieter said nothing, but inwardly he was troubled to the depths of his soul. Teresa wasn't remembering herself right. She had forgotten that her plait should be shorter, because

Lord Xin had sliced it off during their battle on the kitchen shelves.

Hadn't he?

Or was it Amna's charms he'd cut?

But when had that been?

Memory was powerful in the land of the dead, but so too was forgetting. Their souls began to grow faded and worn at the edges like old denim. Perhaps if they had been alone on that long journey, Pieter and Teresa would have lost every part of who they were, memory after memory blown from their heads until they were shapeless will-o'-the-wisps that did not even remember their names.

But it did not happen. They were best friends who knew each other better than summer knows the sun. When Teresa forgot about her plait, Pieter reminded her. When he couldn't remember how he drank his khave, she told him: *half a nib of sugarcane and a smidge of blazing pip.*

"Oh, of course!" he'd say. "And what's this little flickering thing I can see, like a tinderfly stuck behind my eye?"

"That's Amna's fire, which she'll keep lit until we follow it back home."

"I remember now. And am I right in thinking that you're actually a secret princess?"

Teresa's soul blushed blue. "Shut it."

At last, the horizon ahead began to darken, turning from dusk to deepest night. Constellations Pieter had never seen before appeared above them, and the sky glittered with the ghosts of a billion stars that had gone supernova.

The boat surged on, quicker now.

They journeyed into a wide estuary, veering around the sharp reef rocks, then the silt banks, then the dead marsh grass and bubbling mudflats, until the sea became a swamp. Fog surrounded them, thick and cold and gray as old porridge. In the murk they began to see wisps of light in the swamp, drawing closer.

It was Teresa who spotted the first tinderlamps, swinging above the water from the petrified marsh trees like hanged men. Soon, small wooden shacks were appearing, perched up in the bare branches, then finally whole streets of empty houses that teetered on rotting stilts or sat half slumped in the swamp water.

The rowboat bobbed down the silent waterways. And from this city of shrouded windows and leaning doorways, stared the ancient faces of the dead.

2

The Conquering of Catacomb

Every soul had its own shape and color. Wildfolk drifted like wisps of fire smoke, or hung like moonbeams. Laplönder souls seemed to dance in the air, like dust motes in sunlight beneath the everpines. Petrossians glittered, beautiful and cold as icebergs, or swirled like the wind in Worsen.

All the souls that Grim has ever guided, Pieter thought to himself in wonder. *Everyone that ever died in Petrossia . . . he led them here to the land of the dead, and they built themselves a city.*

"Hello?" he called out to them.

The souls shrank back into their houses. They shuttered their windows and put out their lamps.

"Why are they hiding?" Teresa said in the eerie quiet.

A groaning creak made Pieter jump, as a trap door beneath one of the houses swung open. A family of wildfolk souls began drifting down a ladder one at a time onto their moss-covered marsh rafts.

"Hey!" Pieter called.

The wildfolk family crouched down, touching charms in their hair.

"Where are you going?" Pieter asked. "And have you seen a talking skull anywhere?"

A few frightened whispers came back across the water, then the wildfolk started paddling off in the other direction as fast as they could. Soon they were lost in the fog.

"Did you understand them?" he asked Teresa. "What did they say?"

"Warnings," she said, her soul the color of ice. "They told us to leave, and . . . something else. Something I don't understand."

"What?"

"*The czarmy has come*, they said. Not the Czar: the *czarmy*."

The boat drifted on down city canals choked with reeds, gliding under half-sunken walkways and bridges that dripped rust, until finally it bumped against a jetty and scraped to a stop. Grim's hand crawled out, scurried down a passageway, and was soon out of sight. Pieter and Teresa jumped onto the jetty and scrambled after it, following the clack of bone fingertips over the stone floors. There was no other sound. The city was silent and still and shrouded by mist.

Finally, they began to hear faint shouts from up ahead.

The voices were muffled by the fog, but Pieter could still hear the panic in them. Blue flashes lit the passageway as souls flitted across it like bursts of thunder in a cloud: there and then gone. It felt like the moment before a storm. Danger prickled the back of Pieter's neck. Something was happening up ahead, and getting closer . . .

"Pieter, look out!"

Teresa scrambled up a wall to one side, her Spice Monkey skills making her lightning quick. But Pieter was too slow. A torrent of souls was rushing down the passageway toward them, solid and blue as a wave. They plunged straight through him without stopping, their thoughts lodging in his head one after another as he merged with each soul for just an instant.

Run!

The czarmy is in Catacomb!

A sword so sharp it cuts—

Teresa's hand gripped Pieter and hauled him sideways, free of the flood of spirits.

"Their heads were in my head," he gasped. "I heard their thoughts—this city's name is Catacomb. They're fleeing from the Czar."

"Come on!" Teresa gripped his hand and together they jumped back in and forced their way up the passageway, like salmon forging their way upstream. Souls barged straight through them, the panic and wild terror of each one hitting Pieter and Teresa like thunderclaps, until at last they stumbled out onto a wide square plaza.

"Holy Sohcahtoa," Pieter breathed.

The plaza was paved with black and white tiles like a giant chessboard, and lined with grand balconied buildings. This was the center of the Catacomb, where every canal and passageway led.

And it was swarming with czars.

Not just one czar, but *every* czar. All the kings of Petrossia. Every man who had ever worn the Iron Crown.

Teresa yanked Pieter back into the mouth of the shadowy passageway, and together they hid from the glaring pairs of green eyes that each had their own portrait back in the Hall of Faces. Pieter couldn't believe how many there were. Sons, fathers, grandfathers . . . wicked uncles and short-lived nephews . . . hundreds of the foulest souls ever to have lived and died, all gathered in the plaza below.[28]

There was Ivan the Savage, whose teeth were sharpened into points; Boris of the Nine Wives, with his soul like a milky blister ready to pop; Vladimir Beard-cleaver, famous for scalping the chins of his enemies and pinning them

28. The only exception was Nincombob the Brief, the jester who had snatched the Iron Crown and tried it on as a joke and had therefore technically been King of all Petrossia for the seven seconds the Czar had found him amusing enough not to execute.

to his chest like they were medals. Even Tiffany Blood-drinker was there, trying desperately to glue the ghost of a squirrel tail back onto her top lip.

The czars gave up chasing away the last few screaming souls, then drifted back to the plaza, grinning and strutting and fighting over which of them had committed the most massacres when he'd been alive.

"He's brought them all together," Teresa said in awe-struck horror. "An army of czars."

How Pieter wished they had somehow been able to bring Alexander's strength with them, or Amna's magic, or Teresa's alchemy. But what had come in their little boat, across seas and deserts wider than forever? Only him. Just her. Nothing but the two of them, against an entire czarmy.

Suddenly the uproar in the plaza hushed. All the kings turned inward, forming an empty circle at their center. A curved white blade appeared in the middle of the air like a crescent moon, and fell down to the ground in a slash and a slice. A door had appeared, cut from the very fabric of reality. Pieter's soul shook as his mind frantically did the calculations to square-root his fear.

"Ancestors!" boomed a familiar voice.

Through the door, the Czar stepped out onto Catacomb's plaza.

3

The Czarmy

The Czar looked different from when Pieter had seen him last. One tip of his mustache was broken off, like a boar's tusk. Along with his swirling, thunder-flashing, storm-colored soul, that only made him look more fearsome. In the Czar's grasp, the soul-blade had become even more vicious looking than before.

Even the past kings of Petrossia shrunk back from him a little as he appeared. Then they remembered themselves, and launched into deafening roars. They saluted and spat and clapped and beat their hollow chests, each showing approval in their own way. Vladimir Beard-cleaver was so delighted he punched his neighbor in the face and tried to rip off his goatee.

"Catacomb is ours for the taking!" roared the Czar savagely, raising his scimitar blade aloft. "Doesn't conquering make you feel alive again?!"

"If I was alive again," Vladimir Beard-cleaver grumbled, "I'd have a whole new cloak made of my victims' facial hair by now. When will you let someone else have a go with that sharp blade of yours?"

The czarmy made eager sounds of agreement, each of them gazing enviously at the scythe-sword.

The Czar nodded sympathetically. "I hear you, Great-uncle Vladimir. As souls, we can make our enemies *remember* pain—but we cannot truly harm them. It is impossible to kill what has already died. Unless, of course, you hold a soul-blade like I do."

Without warning, the Czar sliced his sword. There was a hideous scream—a sudden dazzling flash. When Pieter opened his eyes, Vladimir Beard-cleaver was on the floor, holding onto his own knotted mustache and sobbing as it dissolved away into nothingness in his hands.

Pieter blinked. He could still see the afterimage of the soul-blade's deadly slice, like a scar behind his eyelids.

"That," growled the Czar, "was for assassinating my father."

"Thanks, son!" a soul called out from the crowd.

"Vladimir Baby-face, as I now rename him, has a point!" called the Czar to the czarmy. "Only when we *all* have swords as sharp as mine will we be a force the land of the dead truly fears! Isn't that right, Grim?"

Pieter and Teresa both clutched each other, as the Czar raised up the skull he had been holding down by his side.

There he was: Petrossia's psychopomp!

Put me back together! Grim snapped. **You promised!**

"Promises are like peace treaties." The Czar grinned. "Made to be broken."

Around him, the czarmy roared with laughter.

You might think you've conquered Death, Grim warned. **But there are other psychopomps—hundreds of them—all guiding souls in lands near and far. You're only ruining Petrossia.**

"Did you hear that?" bellowed the Czar. "Hundreds of others like Grim! And each of them carrying a soul-blade! That is why we must hunt down the psychopomps of Hertz, and Albion, and Madri, and Kiln!"

Grim was so horrified, his jaw dropped.

The Czar picked it up and popped it back into place.

You'll end the worlds! the skull cried, as Pieter and Teresa listened in horror. **Both the lands of the living and the dead! There'll be chaos! Brimstone! Eternal maws of ceaseless horror!**

"Sounds perfect, doesn't it?" said the Czar to his troops. "Now let us hunt down these psychopomps, and soon you will all have swords sharp enough to kill the dead!"

"Huzzah for the Czar of Czars!" yelled the past kings of Petrossia.

Lunatics! Grim shrieked. **Imbeciles! Idi-aaaaaaaahhhh!**

The Czar booted the skull like a ball into the dustiest corner of the plaza, then ordered his czarmy to attention.

"We must go to Coda-in-the-West," he said, "the city where those who die in Hertz are guided to! We will take our second soul-blade from the psychopomp of that land! But no rush. All I need to do to take us there is cut another door in the air." He looked around at his ancestors. "Why don't we enjoy ourselves in Catacomb first? It's been a while since some of you have gone conquering and pillaging." He grinned. "You ought to practice."

Pieter felt a tug on his arm. Teresa pulled him into the gloom of an empty balcony as the czarmy poured out from the plaza and started to ransack the jetties and waterways below them.

"This is the perfect time to attack!" she hissed. "His army's scattered and distracted. It'll be just us versus him."

"You're right!" Pieter glanced up at the plaza, trying to work out a way they could get past the czarmy without being spotted. "Let's hop across the balconies and rescue Grim first. Maybe we can reattach him and send him to warn the other psychopomps."

Teresa seemed about to give him one of her looks. Instead,

she grinned. "I thought you were going to say that attacking the Czar was a crazy and suicidal plan. And probably give me a percentage, too."

"Let's not argue again about whether it's smart or stupid to stand up to a bully," Pieter said, pulling her toward the plaza. "Not when the universe is a fraction away from ending."

Around the plaza's edge they crept, darting from balcony to balcony, sliding down the slopes of dust piled up around the ruined buildings. Around them it was chaos. The czarmy smashed and thrashed and trashed their way through Catacomb. Screams and splashes and tremors and crashes echoed through the fog.

Ahead of them, Tiffany Blood-drinker swaggered past. They hid in a doorway until her squirrel-tail mustache fell off, and she bent down to pick it up. Then they were sprinting round her and skidding behind the piles of dust in the plaza corner where the Czar had booted Grim.

Grim's skeletal hand was already there, digging out his skull. It grinned at them, half-buried. Pieter picked it up carefully and gave the skull a shake. Dust streamed out of it, like sand from a timer, leaving one single yellow speck stuck in the center of each eye socket. The specks turned yellow to pink when they saw Pieter.

You're the boy who got his head snipped off on Yuletide

day. How did you get here? I never fetched you. The eyes flicked to Teresa. **Or you.**

"Actually, part of you *did* fetch us." Pieter pointed at the hand scurrying beneath Grim's skull like a puppy being reunited with its owner.

Grim looked down at his hand, eyes flaring up in surprise. **Wow!** he said sarcastically. **Well done, Lefty. There's a maniac running around Catacomb, waving around my soul-blade, and you bring two children to sort things out. No wonder I only use you for two-handed tasks.**

"We can deal with the Czar!" Pieter said, peering over the mound of dust to check where he was. He couldn't find him in the fog: the plaza was too crowded.

You two? Deal with the Czar? Grim's jaw clacked open and shut as he laughed.

Teresa scowled. Her hand shot forward and angled Grim's skull up toward her. Anger rumbled inside her spring thunderstorm-colored soul.

"I am Teresa Gust," she said. "Alchemaster and Heir to the Iron Crown. This is Pieter Abadabacus: he knows his fifty-seven times table. We have come a very long way to sort out a problem that only started when your idea of dealing with the Czar was getting yourself broken up into bits and thrown in a sack. And that was when you had the sharpest blade in the universe on a big stick."

Grim's jaw clacked open. **Ouch**, he said. **If I had facial muscles, they'd be wincing. That was a good speech.**

Teresa shrugged. "I practiced. It was a long boat ride."

Time well spent. See, that's what the Czar doesn't understand about the land of the dead. Power here doesn't just lie in swords—

"It's in *words*," Pieter interrupted. "Memories too. We've already figured that out."

"Did we mention," said Teresa, "that we're both geniuses?"

Grim seemed to take a second look at them both. **Geniuses with a mad, brilliant idea to save the universe?** he asked hopefully.

Teresa looked at Pieter. "Wait five minutes while we put our heads together," she told Grim.

In the end, they had the plan all figured out after three.

Is it mad? Grim asked.

Teresa nodded. "A little."

Brilliant?

Pieter shrugged. "Undoubtedly."

Will it save the universe?

The two friends looked at each other. "There's a chance," they both said.

Grim's grin seemed to somehow stretch wider. **Tell me.**

4

The Most Powerful Weapon of All

Across the plaza, Pieter and Teresa and Grim went hunting through the fog for the Czar. They had no ally but the skull in their hands and no weapon but the single mad, brilliant idea in their heads. The space where Pieter's heart used to beat was thudding like a hollow drum; the ghosts of his nerves were tingling. Yet the plan in his mind was clear and strong. And the first part of it was simply: *Find the Czar.*

"That him?" Pieter pointed to a figure up ahead. They crept closer . . . but it was only Ivan the Savage, grinning like a devil as he kicked stilts out from beneath a plaza building. Trapped on the balconies above him, a family of Laplönder souls wailed and wobbled as they started to teeter down toward the swamp . . .

Then suddenly it was Ivan who was screaming, as Pieter crept up behind him, and held Grim aloft.

CHOMP.

His victims up on the balcony cheered as the vicious king hopped around the plaza, shrieking and weeping and trying to pry a skull off his bottom.

Pieter and Teresa did not stop to celebrate. They searched on, until Boris of the Nine Wives lumbered into their path. He was carrying his newly engaged tenth bride through the fog, despite the fact that she was hitting him over the head with her shoe and screaming, "I SAID NO!"

He lunged for Teresa, crying out, "And here's number eleven!" but she ran up his arms like they were kitchen shelves, then plunged her hand into his hollow head and stirred his thoughts until he fell over with confusion. Boris's Would-Be Tenth Wife stood up, gave them a look of eternal gratitude, then ran off.

"Oi!" Pieter yelled.

The Czar stood with his back to them, only ten paces away. He was busy cutting an enormous portal in the air for all his men to march through. Just the corner of it had been done.

When Pieter's voice echoed across the plaza, he froze. Very slowly, he turned around and held up his sword. Mist drifted across the sharp edge of the soul-blade, curling in the air in long shaved spirals.

In other tales, less true than this one, the Czar might stop and deliver a long and gloating speech to Pieter and Teresa, giving them the time or the information they needed to defeat him. But he said nothing to them. He did not ask how they had come to Catacomb, or if they knew of his plan. He just came forward, silent and cold-eyed, to kill them.

Teresa and Pieter were quick but the Czar was quicker. He whipped the soul-blade up and slashed it down so fast that there was no way they could dodge it. It would slice them even if they rolled to the side, or ducked, or jumped back. There was no way of dodging that deadly strike.

But that didn't matter.

Dodging wasn't part of the plan.

Pieter knelt down, and Teresa stood on his knee and launched herself into the path of the blade.

And just before it cut them both in two, her hand reached up and her fingertips brushed the Czar's face.

There was a white flash and a mighty thunderclap sound as the two stormy souls of father and daughter met. In the instant they connected, Teresa called up one single memory from the deepest depths of her soul, and sent it to the Czar.

Pieter gasped as he saw an image bloom in both their heads like a dazzling flower.

It truly was the greatest weapon in all Petrossia, just as all the stories had said.

Inches from Pieter's neck, the soul-blade slowed to a stop, as if it had become a blunt spoon and the fog was old porridge that would not be stirred. Then the sword slipped from the Czar's limp grip and clattered on the plaza beside him.

In one anguished howl, all the rage and bluster of his thunderous soul burst out of him. In his chest, a hole appeared like the eye of a storm. Teresa had just reopened the oldest, deepest, only wound the Czar's soul had ever suffered.

Suddenly he was sobbing, great torrential tears falling from his eyes, falling and falling and falling. Teresa was crying too, silent and still like a statue of a saint. In both their minds, Pieter saw the memory slowly wilt away and vanish: the greatest weapon in Petrossia.

The only thing that had ever conquered the Czar, that Teresa had carried within her since the moment she had been born.

Her mother's all-conquering smile.

Pieter picked up the soul-blade by the broken scythe-handle grip. The Czar cringed away from him, his sniveling soul the weak-gray color of dirty puddles.

"Wait!" shrieked the Czar. "I'll make you my heir! I'll

give you your very own soul-blade! Anything you want you can have! I'll conquer it and give it to you."

"End it, Pieter," said Teresa through her tears, fists clenched. "You know what we do to bullies."

And Pieter raised the sword: for Teresa, for the Czarina, for Amna and the Baba Sisters, and everyone else. But the blade never came down.

"No," he said.

Triumph flashed across the Czar's face—confusion filled Teresa's.

"I was wrong," Pieter told her. "You can survive bullies for a bit, but not forever. And you were wrong too, Teresa. You can stand up to them sometimes, but not always. Because I've just realized something."

Before she could speak, he took the sword-blade and cut a letterbox-sized hole in the air. Then he posted it through, not knowing or caring where in the universe it was, and sealed the letterbox shut.

"The smart choice," he said, "is just to walk away and be done with them. Forever."

Then he took her by the hand and led her over the plaza, leaving the Czar alone. In the corners of their eyes, a faint glimmer burned like a distant star, calling them home. They followed it, and neither one of them looked back.

As Pieter and Teresa walked off into the mist, the Czar staggered to his feet. He clutched at the hole in the center of his soul and moaned. How it hurt, all over again, fresh as the day she had died! What had that girl done to him? Revenge! He needed revenge!

"Come back here!" he screamed at their backs. "I am the Czar! I ruled from the Boreal Sea to the Western Woodn't! I wore the Iron Crown! A hundred armies did my bidding! No one turns away from me!"

But he was screaming at the emptiness. Teresa and Pieter were out of sight now. He stood alone on the empty plaza.

"I'll find the soul-blade again!" he roared. "Wherever it went, I'll search for it! The whole land of the dead if I have to! I've got all eternity, haven't I?" He began to chuckle to himself. "You haven't beaten me. No one ever has. I'm the mightiest conqueror of all."

But the frightening thing was, he didn't *feel* mighty. Not anymore. What power did he hold now, without the sword?

"Czarmy!" he called out across the plaza. "Troops, I summon you! I order you to gather here! Ivan the Savage! Boris? Igor?"

A few figures gradually stumbled back on the plaza and gathered around him, but they did not have the same conquering look he had seen earlier. They looked frightened. Boris was holding his head and staggering, and Ivan the Savage was trying to pry Grim's skull off his bottom.

"Czar of Czars!" Igor began. "The city, it—"

"Forget Catacomb!" said the Czar.

"But—"

"SILENCE!" He had to get his authority back. He squared his shoulders and crossed his arms over his chest, hoping it would hide the wound in his soul. "Find my soulblade! Find it no*owwwwwww*!"

His speech ended in a scream as, out of the murky fog, a low blue shape leaped onto his back. It tore at him, teeth and claws, until the Czar fell backwards and shook it off. The creature did a somersault across the plaza and scrabbled back on its paws.

It was Bloodbath.

The poodle bared its jaws and growled.

If I had shoulders, said Grim, as he dropped off Ivan's bottom with a plonk, **I'd be shrugging them. Maybe Bloodbath put in a request for a haunting when he died. Maybe it was a request to haunt you. Maybe a lot of the victims that you and all the other czars conquered all did the same. Maybe the line was decades long. And maybe I just granted all those requests at once.**

The Czar became aware that the swamp beneath them was trembling now. The sound of footsteps approaching. Down onto the plaza, through the fog, blue spirits were marching. Rushing toward the czarmy like a waterfall. Hundreds—no, thousands—no, hundreds of thousands. Row upon row, and all of them aglow. In every shade of blue, from sky to sea to sapphire. Every victim of every czar, every soul ever conquered.

All come to settle their unfinished business.

Babapatra, with charms swinging in her long dreadlocked hair. Eight Baba Sister brides beside her. King Harollia of Laplönd. Nincombob the Brief. Even the Czar's own Great-aunt Anastasia . . .

And then the Czar saw the Czarina, her soul the color of spring rain, holding a ghostly bunch of mintflower.

And beside her were two mathemagicians, wearing necklaces of abacus beads, their hair curled into long Fibonacci spirals.

And as one they opened their mouths and started to sing:

"Done and dusted, you're no King,
No power over anything.
You killed us when we were alive,
So see that swamp? GO TAKE A DIVE!"

They sang together, in a single vast voice that was louder than anything the Czar had ever heard. He raised up his fists, but the army of souls washed over him like a tidal wave, and swept him and his czarmy off the plaza and into the marsh with a splash.

No one ever saw the Czar again. But for thousands of years to come, those in Catacomb would sometimes glimpse in the swamp around the city a will-o'-the-wisp shape of a lost soul. Those who got near enough to see it clearly, said that it was so old it had forgotten its shape and how to speak. There was no way of asking who it had once been, or what it was searching for, endlessly and without success, amongst the marsh reeds.

5

Two Farewells, One Happy and One Sad

That was the end of the Czar. But, of course, it was not the end of the story. There isn't one. There is only a place where your telling stops, while the story goes on without you, regardless.

And so, after Pieter and Teresa searched the city for the soul of an anatomist to help piece Grim back together—

After they'd chased his fluttering cloak around the plaza until the wind let them catch it—

After Grim took up his job as psychopomp once more, and found his soul-blade using the compass in his scythe-handle—

The time came for Pieter and Teresa to say goodbye.

Grim led the way back to the land of living. He clicked and popped his joints as he stood up on the plaza, a skeleton once more, gripping the scythe in his bony hands. He motioned for all the souls to stand back as he cut a door in the air, and pulled it open.

Shortcut, he said.

Light blazed behind it, sudden and blinding, so bright that Pieter could barely look at it. And yet at the same time he could not tear his gaze away, it was so beautiful. It was amazing how quickly he had forgotten how blue the sky could be. Through the doorway was the Winter Palace courtyard. There was the fire, still burning. There was Alexander, curled up and asleep. There was Amna, gray and slumped with exhaustion, still feeding the flames with the last bits of kindling.

And there were Pieter and Teresa: his head still on the velvet cushion beside the fire, and her lying beside him. But both of their bodies were empty. It was strange how Pieter could tell. It was like looking at a glass bottle full of water, and then coming back later to find someone had poured it down the sink. The water might have been clear, the glass bottle itself might not look any different . . . and yet you still knew that there was something missing.

Come, said Grim. **Let me lead you back to where you belong.**

But as they stepped forward, Grim held out his hand.

Not you, Pieter.

In the back of his mind, Pieter had always known this moment was coming. He had no life to go back to. It had ended on Yuletide day.

"No," Teresa said, clutching at him. "No, that's not *fair*!"

It's completely fair, said Grim. **There are rules.**

"But he *saved* Petrossia!" Teresa shouted. "He got you your scythe back! He's my best friend! He . . ."

He *died*, Grim reminded her gently.

"Teresa," Pieter said quietly. "It's okay."

She gave him one of her looks (the one she never gave to anyone else, before or after). Then she wiped jewel-blue tears from her eyes, and hugged him tight.

There was nothing to say. Maybe if things had been different, they could have grown up together. Somewhere there is a great long list of all the things that ended far too soon, and written on it are the words "Pieter and Teresa's friendship."

6
Unfinished Business

It was strange. Life and Death had finally been fixed, but now it was Pieter who felt broken. He'd lost his life before he'd lived it, and he was miserable.

He took a little stilt house at the edge of the city and its fog, and sat at the window, counting dead stars to pass the time.

I could take you to Elucid, the skeleton said one night when he came to visit. **It is the city the Eurekans built, after their psychopomp Azreal brought them to the land of the dead. I know your parents have not returned there yet. They've been here ever since the Czar was defeated. I'm told they are searching for you.**

His mother and father? Pieter didn't want to see *them*. When they had appeared on the plaza to sweep away the czarmy, he had gone away and hid. How could he ever forget how they had abandoned him?

I'm sure I don't need to tell a mathemagician, said Grim,

what the odds are that you can avoid them forever. And I'm certain too that someone who has dabbled in alchemy like *you* have already knows that people can change.

"Family," Pieter said, the ghost of a headache groaning in his head. "Now there's a problem that no formula will ever solve. But I suppose you're right. I should try and work it out anyway."

I'll be sad to see you go, Grim said. **There's an enormous backlog of souls to collect in Petrossia. I can barely keep up with *today's* deaths, let alone the deaths from Yule and spring that are still waiting to happen. . . .**

Pieter looked at the skeleton suspiciously. "Wait a second."

What? The pupils in Grim's twin eye sockets shone with twinkly innocence.

"This sounds as if you're about to offer me a job, Grim."

Grim's jaw clacked open and shut rapidly, like a pair of wind-up teeth. It took Pieter a moment to realize the skeleton was laughing.

Offer you a job? As my assistant? Not if you were the last soul in Catacomb! You indirectly murdered the last person who employed you.

"But you're already a skeleton," said Pieter, trying not to sound hurt, "so that wouldn't be such an issue. . . ."

Grim leaned on his scythe. **You don't want to work for**

me, Pieter. You've got unfinished business. You want to go back and live again, don't you?

Pieter felt his blue soul blush. "Is it really that obvious?"

I can see right through you, Pieter. Literally.

He sighed and slumped onto the plaza, hugging his knees. "I *know* it's impossible—" he began, but Grim cut him off.

Don't be ridiculous. Of *course* it's possible. *Anything* is. It's just not *allowed*. Souls go from Life to Death—never the other way. I almost didn't get permission to let Teresa go home.

"Right."

I had to fill out a whole bunch of forms.

"I see."

And make an appeal.

"Oh."

Life and Death have *very* strict rules on these things.

Grim's red gaze started to flicker amber, then a mischievous green.

Fate, however . . . Well Fate is *much* more willing to make exceptions. Complete romantic, She is, in my opinion. Which is why, when it came to you, I put in your request straight to Her.

"Request?"

From the black folds of his robe, Grim took out a scroll and held it out. It looked very official—there was a black wax seal and silver-gilt paper.

If I had eyebrows, they'd be waggling up and down right now.

Pieter just looked even more confused.

For a genius, you sure are fond of explanations, said Grim with a sigh, unrolling it from the bottom upwards. **It's an *Asking*, Pieter. This is just how *we* see it, of course.**

On the form, in scrawly black handwriting, Grim had written out Pieter's name, his date of birth (and death), and every other detail about him.

"Is this . . ." Pieter looked up breathlessly. "Is this a haunting request?"

No, said Grim. **Better than that.**

Typed at the top of the form was:

!!! APPLICATION FOR EMERGENCY REINCARNATION !!!

And at the bottom, stamped in red, was the word:

APPROVED

It hadn't been easy for Grim. He'd been determined to

repay Pieter for his part in defeating the Czar, but bringing people back to life wasn't exactly his area of expertise.

To pull it off, he needed help.

And so it was that, a week after she'd returned to the Winter Palace, Teresa found a very tall, very thin man in a hooded cloak waiting by her bed when she woke.

"What do you want?" she said to Grim, arms folded. She still hadn't forgiven him for what he'd done to her best friend.

I've got a problem on my hands, he began. **Called Pieter Abadabacus.**

Teresa's scowl became a smile. "Well, that's a problem I'm happy to help you solve."

And so Grim explained his plan. The biggest issue was this: Pieter's old life was gone, and so he needed a new one. But lives are precious things—as far as Grim knew, there weren't many knocking around to spare.

"Sure there are," Teresa interrupted. "Cats have nine of them, don't they?"

Grim stood up. **Then I think we need an audience with the Empurrer.**

At first, Teresa had tried to work out a way to weaken and dilute the Catastrophica potion in Alexander, so that her little brother might change back into a boy. It was hard.

Teresa was good at making alchemy, not reversing it, and the Catastrophica had been made to last. She searched Blüstav's books for ways to weaken the potion, but she soon gave up. It was clear that Alexander was quite happy being a gentle, friendly, and rather lazy cat, who liked snoozing, having his belly rubbed, and playing hide-and-seek with Petrossian children dressed up as mice.

The people of Petrossia were delighted with him: everyone agreed that he was the best ruler they had ever had. Because he was so huge, Alexander scared away the marauding Mongols or barbarians. And because he was a cat, there was no more need for serfs to serve in his palace, or soldiers to fight in his wars: the Empurrer was happy to sleep in a giant wicker basket, as big as a barn, and drink from a pond-sized saucer of milk.

The only problem was keeping Alexander well fed, but it was Teresa who provided the solution to his appetite. After many days, and over a dozen extra ingredients, she whipped up another batch of Gargantua potion. Then she walked with her brother down to the River Ossia every morn, crouched by the hole he poked in the ice, and with a fishing rod (the same one the Czar had used to conquer King Harollia) caught a fish.

With a sprinkle of Gargantua, the fish became the size of a

whale, and the people of Petrossia were saved from starvation.

Alexander happily gave up one of his nine lives for Pieter to have. He had eight others to live, after all, and by the time he came to the end of his last one, he had grown into a gentle, sleepy old cat, and Petrossia had become a gentle, sleepy old kingdom. In history books, his reign is known as The Long Snooze, for it was the loveliest and dreamiest and most contented time in Petrossia's history, and Empurrer Alexander is often called the Purrfect.

But no historians mention anything called Operation: *His Royal Whiskers.*

So I got you a second life, Grim said to Pieter in the city of Catacomb. ***Alexander's*** **second life, to be precise.** He poked the scroll with a bony finger. **All you need to do is sign on the dotted line. If you want it, that is.**

Pieter didn't think he could ever want anything more. When a quill appeared in Grim's fingers, he snatched for it at once, but the skeleton whipped it back.

Wait, he said. **There's a catch.**

When it comes to contracts (and life in general) there always is.

The catch was this: if Pieter chose life, he would have to start it from the beginning.

The very beginning.

As an ickle-wickle baby.

He wouldn't be able to take much with him. A baby's head is like a very tiny suitcase, with not much room for luggage. There'd be just enough space to pack a few memories and feelings, or maybe a single First Word. That would be all.

Everything else, he'd have to leave behind: his memories, his name, his fifty-seven times table . . .

Resurrection wasn't an option, said Grim. **I did check, but it's almost Swoon now and your old body has gotten sort of . . . squishy. So what'll it be? It's time you left Catacomb, one way or the other.**

Pieter looked at the contract. He looked at the horizon, toward Elucid. Then back at the dotted line on the contract. Which line should he choose?

To answer, he looked inside himself. He wondered which memories he would take, and which he would leave behind. He thought of his triumphs and regrets. His rights and wrongs.

In the end though, it wasn't any of that which made Pieter decide to go back. It was remembering a blue door of sky, with a girl standing in it, and that moment, which had seemed to last longer than the rest of his life, when they had looked at each other, wondering what might have been.

7

The End and the Start

When the baby came, Amnabushka and Elsie Peppercorn were too busy playing dominoes to notice. They sat in their trundle wagon—two old ladies with their slippered feet propped up by the roaring stove—whilst the storm shook the shutters and rain rattled on the tin roof. Outside, the waves heaved themselves one by one onto Albion's shore, an endless cycle of dump, drown, and dissolve upon the shingle. Blue flashes lit the nets on the table that Elsie mended for the fishermen. Thunder rattled the lid on the teapot.

They remembered all of this later, when wondering why they hadn't heard the door open. It was simpler to blame the racket of a storm than to consider the other possibility—that the door had not opened at all—that the monk had just *appeared* in the middle of the room with the child.

The monk (he had to be a monk, for who else wears

such long hooded robes?) had held out his pale, slender hands.

"Almost white, they were," Elsie would tell the fishermen the next morning. "I bet he hardly ever leaves the monastery."

A baby lay there, in the cradle of the monk's grasp. A little squalling bundle. Raging storm in miniature.

Please make him stop, pleaded the monk. (Such a voice he had! He must have picked it up from talking with the angels.)

Elsie and Amna got up from their dominoes. They started to ask the monk who he was, and why he was there, and how he managed to walk through the storm without getting a single raindrop on his robe, but somehow when they saw the baby, their questions just disintegrated into a sounds of *Ooh! Aah! Coochy-coochy-coo!*

And the baby boy stopped crying.

Thank the Universe, said the monk. **And I thought he was irritating *before* he reincarnated.**

"Teresa," said the baby.

Elsie and Amna stopped blowing raspberries and wiggling their noses. Their silly faces went slack. They blinked in astonishment. The boy looked barely hours old, and already he could *talk*?

Just that word, said the monk, although neither Elsie nor Amna had spoken out loud. **He absolutely refused to forget it.**

"Amna knows a Teresa up in Barter town," said Elsie in wonder. "She's apprenticed to Alchemaster Blüstav."

"We sailed over the Boreal Sea together last summer," Amna explained.

"My Amna came with her," gabbled Elsie. "All the way from Petrossia! I was by the harbor when they first came ashore, mending nets."

"Ensnared me, she did," said Amna, touching a new fish-hook charm in her hair, and cackling when Elsie blushed.

The monk interrupted with a sigh. **Yes, yes. I know all about you two. And Teresa. That's why he asked to be born here. Obviously there'll be an age gap, but not so big that . . . well. You can tell him. You're his parents, after all.**

Before Elsie and Amna could say anything in reply, the monk had tipped the baby into their arms.

"Teresa," said the baby happily, as an indescribably awful smell wafted up from its nappy.

Wow, said the monk. **I don't even have a nose, and that still stinks. I'm off.**

"Off? What do you mean, you're off?" said Elsie. Amna

didn't say anything because she had gone over to the stove to change the baby.

Look, said the monk. **I know this is strange. To be honest, the two of you were destined to always wish for a child but never be granted one. And then you were both going to die after eating a bad omelet.** The monk paused, as if mentally checking something. **Yeah, that's still gonna happen. But the child thing has changed. So I can understand this is a bit of a shock, but—**

"Elsie!" Amna called out happily. "Help me change him!"

"But wait!" said Elsie, turning to the monk. "What's the lad's name?"

The monk had already gone. (He really did open and close doors *very* quickly.) Strangely, Elsie still heard him speak.

His name's Daffodil.

Then:

Only joking. He didn't choose to remember his name. Only hers. Call him whatever you like.

Outside, the weather still seethed and spat. Inside Amna and Elsie's wagon, the tiny storm that had entered their lives that night was burbling happily in his new mother's arms.

"Teresa," he murmured sleepily.

"Say Amna," said his mum.

"Teresa."

"He's a clever little mite." Elsie grinned. "Could even be a genius."

Amna touched the abacus bead tied in her hair. "Truly? Then we should name him Pieter."

Elsie scrunched up her face as she inspected the baby. "He doesn't look like a Peter. Besides, Peter Peppercorn? What is he, a tongue twister? Can't give a boy a name like that. They'll tease him at school. Looks like a Henry to me."

"Henry Peppercorn," Amna murmured, looking down at the little boy in her arms. "*Many miles may you live.*"

"Sing him a song," Elsie said. "Send him off to beddy-byes."

Amna smiled. "Make a babbi sleep? That's magic beyond what I know."

Elsie grinned and said, "Tell him a bedtime story, then. Stimulate his brain."

"A story?" said Amna.

"From Petrossia," said Elsie, settling back into her chair and throwing wood into the stove. "And I'll listen too."

"A story from Petrossia . . ." Amna closed her eyes and thought. She only really knew one. It was rather gruesome for a baby, but then their little Henry Peppercorn was a genius, and besides, it had a happy ending of sorts, and no one truly died in it.

"*Bloom and Swoon and many a moon ago,*" Amna began, "*in the lands beyond the Boreal Sea, there lived a mighty king who loved conquering. He conquered crowns and cities and countries. His name was the Czar . . .*"

The End

Acknowledgments

So many thank-yous, great and small:

My agents, Becky Bagnell and Allison Hellegers at Rights People and Lindsay Literary Agency. My editors, Charlie Sheppard and Chloe Sackur, along with Annie Nybo at Margaret K. McElderry Books. You grew this story with me, and turned it from catastrophe to purr-fection. Your skills at alchemy never cease to amaze me.

Sydney Hansen—you had the impossibly gruesome job of illustrating a severed skeletal fist in a children's book, and you executed said task brilliantly.

Debra Sfetsios-Conover—you made this book look sharp as a guillotine blade.

Sue Cook—thanks for chopping away the spelling mistakes.

My early readers: Sarah, Erin, Mum—who encouraged me to advance ever onward.

Ms. Tysall—who first inspired me with tales of Czarist Russia.

And finally to Helen Vjestica, from Brewood CE Middle School in Staffordshire, who came up with the title of His Royal Whiskers four years ago when I started this story. Thank you for giving me permission to magpie your title.

If czars have War Councils, then authors have Story Councils. Thank you, all. Here's to the next conquest.